THE
MOTOR MAIDS
IN
FAIR JAPAN

KATHERINE STOKES

1st WORLD
LIBRARY
Literary Society

The Motor Maids in Fair Japan

Katherine Stokes

© 1st World Library – Literary Society, 2004
PO Box 2211
Fairfield, IA 52556
www.1stworldlibrary.org
First Edition

LCCN: 2005901344

Softcover ISBN: 1-4218-1159-6
Hardcover ISBN: 1-4218-1059-X
eBook ISBN: 1-4218-1259-2

Purchase *"The Motor Maids in Fair Japan"*
as a traditional bound book at:
www.1stWorldLibrary.org/purchase.asp?ISBN=1-4218-1159-6

1st World Library Literary Society is a nonprofit
organization dedicated to promoting literacy by:

- Creating a free internet library accessible from any computer worldwide.
- Hosting writing competitions and offering book publishing scholarships.

Readers interested in supporting literacy
through sponsorship, donations or
membership please contact:
literacy@1stworldlibrary.org
Check us out at: www.1stworldlibrary.ORG
and start downloading free ebooks today.

The Motor Maids in Fair Japan
contributed by Tim, Ed & Rodney
in support of
1st World Library Literary Society

CONTENTS

CHAPTER I.

OFF FOR JAPAN.

"The Motor Maids are off again," announced the West Haven Courier one morning, as if every citizen in the gray old town on the coast was not already well aware of it.

The four famous travelers and their chaperone, Miss Helen Campbell, were always off somewhere in the red motor car. If they were not making a voyage to England with the "Comet" stored in the hold of the ship for immediate use on arrival, or taking perilous journeys across the American continent in the faithful car, they were making excursions to Shell Island or Seven League Island, or down the coast to the Sailors' Inn.

"Where is it to be this time, Nancy-Bell?" Captain Brown had asked his daughter when she had broken the news to him that she must give up the spring term at High School for something far more educational than mere books. Perhaps the sea captain had intended to be stern when he asked that question; but Nancy had her own peculiar methods of dispelling sternness. A beaming anticipatory smile irradiated her face and scattered parental disapproval even as the warm rays of the sun scatter the morning mists.

"Japan!" she announced solemnly; and Captain Brown, who himself had made voyages to Japan in his youth, pricked up his ears like an old hunting dog when he hears the call of the pack. The name of High School faded from his memory. It was the high seas he was thinking of - the great desert of waters, the fresh salt breeze and the foam track left by the little ship as it cut through the waves.

Without a word, he opened an old sea chest and drew out an atlas and chart. Nancy blinked her eyes and smiled happily. She wondered if the other girls were having as easy a time in breaking the amazing news to their parents. Would Elinor Butler's father and mother consent to her taking this long journey? Would Mrs. Price be willing to part with Mary for many, many months while that young person journeyed to the other side of the world? Captain Brown settled himself on a settee in front of the crackling driftwood fire and Nancy seated herself beside him.

"You see, it's this way, father," she began, while Captain Brown turned the leaves of the atlas with reverent fingers. "Billie Campbell's father is a great engineer -"

"I've known him since he was a boy, child," interrupted the Captain.

"He's been invited by the Japanese government to go to Japan on some consulting work, and he says he can't live without Billie another summer, and Billie says she can't exist without us; so Mr. Campbell is to take a house in Tokyo and we are all to go. Mr. Ignatius Donahue is going to take us across to San Francisco in his private car. He says it's a very small return for something we did for him once, and the end of the story is that we are to sail for Japan in two weeks. Isn't that delightful, Captain Brown?" she added, giving her father a tight hug and kissing him on the end of his nose. "And aren't you overjoyed for your little daughter to have such an opportunity to see the other side of the world?"

The Captain returned the kiss with good measure and resumed his study of the maps and charts.

"You'll be a member of the Royal Geographical Society next," he observed.

"It's all happened because Billie Campbell has a mole on the sole of her left foot and a Gypsy once told her that was the mark of the wanderer."

"But you and Elinor and Mary haven't any moles on the soles of your feet, have you?"

"No, and neither has Miss Campbell."

"It's just as well," commented the Captain. "One is enough in the party if it's going to take my little daughter away from her home most of the time."

"Not most of the time, father," protested Nancy. "Only to Palm Beach and across the Continent and to England -"

At this dangerous turn in the conversation, the door was pushed open and Billie Campbell rushed in, followed by Elinor Butler and Mary Price.

"It's all settled, Nancy-Bell," she cried. "Cousin Helen has consented and the girls can go. Everything depends on you, now -"

"We are just studying the map," answered Nancy quickly, with a demure smile.

Immediately the other girls seated themselves in a circle about the sea captain and his charts, and Mrs. Brown, whose consent had already been gained, presently appeared with a large platter of cookies.

So it was that the Motor Maids and Miss Campbell sailed through the Golden Gate of San Francisco harbor one morning en route for the island empire of Japan. On the long and sometimes tedious voyage we will not dwell; nor shall we pause until we have left them on the piazza of their new home in Tokyo, while seven Japanese servants are making profound obeisances at the entrance and their attendant families, including three grandmothers and five funny little children, bob and bow in the rear of this formidable company.

Billie, who had scarcely left her father's side since the joyful moment of their reunion, hung on his arm and smiled up into his face inquiringly; while Miss Helen Campbell, his cousin, exclaimed:

"Dear me, Duncan; I thought we were to stay at a private house - not a hotel."

Mr. Campbell, from his mysterious dwelling places in far distant lands, had made so many things possible for the Motor Maids that Billie's three friends had come to regard him as a kind of powerful spirit who had only to will things to happen and they happened. At first they were rather shy of the real Mr. Campbell, big and strong and splendid, the very image of his daughter, Billie, if she had grown half a foot and cropped her light brown hair closely all over her head.

"But, Cousin Helen, this is a private house," answered this human presentment of the good spirit, a subdued humor lighting his gray eyes, exactly as they had seen Billie's eyes kindle hundreds of times. "This is your very own villa and this is your staff of domestics," he added, indicating the regiment of servants who again bowed low like the chorus in a comic opera. "You are to regard yourself as queen of this little realm," he went on, pointing to the charming grounds and garden surrounding the house, "and you are to be in absolute command. Nellie and Nannie and Mollie and Billie are to be your maids of honor and I'll be general factotum and protector. As for the staff," he continued in a whisper, "their combined wages for one month amount to about one good servant's hire at home."

The maid in the front of the cohort now stepped forth. She was much older than the others; her hair was short and her blue cotton robe seemed severe and plain in comparison to the gay colored kimonos of the younger maids.

"This is our housekeeper and cook, O'Haru San," announced Mr. Campbell.

"I shall leave you in her charge now and keep an appointment."

So saying, Mr. Duncan Campbell kissed his daughter, smiled delightfully on the company in general and hastened down the walk to the road, for the villa was in the suburbs of Tokyo.

"Will honorable ladies enter humble, small house," said O'Haru making an obeisance.

But before they could move an inch, the maids were at their feet deftly unfastening their shoes.

"What in the world are they doing?" demanded Miss Campbell.

"One never wears shoes in the house, Cousin, don't you remember? Papa told us so this morning," answered Billie slipping her feet into the straw sandals provided.

"Perfect nonsense!" exclaimed Miss Campbell, shuffling into the hall in her loose footgear. "I suppose I shall be expected to sit on the floor and eat my meals on a door mat," she complained, "and that I positively will not do. My old joints are far too stiff to be doubled up like a pair of nut crackers."

The girls giggled and the four little Japanese maids giggled, too; not that they understood a word of the language, but good humor is the keynote of the Japanese character and strangers are treated with a sympathetic courtesy and hospitality unequaled in any other country.

However, Miss Campbell's fears were immediately set at rest, for the long, low-ceiled drawing-room of the villa was furnished in European fashion with plenty of comfortable arm-chairs and sofas made of bamboo. The floors were covered with thick soft mats and the front walls facing the piazza were really sliding panels covered with opaque paper through which the light cast a soft mellow luster. As a matter of fact, Dr. and Mrs. Spears, the owners of the villa, had kept it as Japanese as possible without interfering with their foreign ideas of comfort. The only ornaments were several beautiful scrolls and screens and a few vases.

Instead of sitting down quietly and being served to tea, which was evidently the next duty expected of them by these formal domestics, Billie and her friends rushed from one room to another in a state of eager curiosity. They poked their inquisitive little noses into the charming bedrooms and even peeped into the mysterious kitchen quarters where O'Haru reigned supreme,

"It's Japanese enough to be pretty and American enough to be comfortable," observed Nancy, arranging her curls at one of the bedroom mirrors.

"I don't know why you call it 'American,'" objected Billie. "I think you should say 'international,' since beds may be imported from Turkey, Russia, Prussia, England, or France, to say nothing of Germany and Italy."

"Well, no matter what nationality it is, I'm glad I'm going to sleep on a bed instead of on the floor as Japanese girls do, with a little bench for a pillow to keep from rumpling my hair."

Just then a Japanese girl appeared in the doorway. She was quite young, perhaps seventeen, perhaps older, and enchantingly pretty.

"Her eyes are like stewed prunes," wrote Nancy to her mother that night, "rich and black and luscious. Her hair is as black as father's ebony box and quite as shiny; her skin smooth and creamy. She has a little rosebud mouth and a small straight nose and she wore the most beautiful kimono, all blue with a cerise sash or *obi*, as it is called. Her name is 'Onoye' and she's the daughter of the cook, O'Haru. She is just one of the maids in the house, I suppose, but she seems better class and she speaks a little English. Her mother adores her and I suppose Onoye is being spoiled Japanese fashion, which is very different from American fashion. Japanese girls are the most unselfish, uncomplaining, considerate, everything-that-I'm-not little souls I ever saw."

Nancy's description of O'Haru's daughter was not exaggerated in the least. Little Onoye, pausing timidly at the entrance to their bedroom, was a vision to charm the eye. She blushed, smiled deprecatingly and hung her head.

"Will honorable ladies be pleased to employ humble refreshment?" she announced in a funny high voice with a prim, precise accent.

The girls would have laughed if it had not been impolite. All their impulsive actions must be checked in this land of perfect manners, or they would certainly appear rude and rough.

"We should be most pleased and happy, I am sure," answered Billie, feeling that she must not be outdone in lofty expression, "But what excellent English you speak. Do you live here, too?"

Onoye looked up and her face brightened.

"I make studying of American language one time," she said.

"And are we to have tea now?" asked Nancy as the Japanese girl backed out of the room.

"If pleasingly to gracious ladies," she answered.

With bobs and bows, she led the way to a summer house in the garden where the others were already installed in comfortable chairs.

"These are certainly the most hospitable servants I ever saw,"

Miss Campbell was saying to Mary and Elinor. "They make one feel like a guest in one's own house. I am sure if I lived here long, I should learn to meet myself at the front door and invite myself to take refreshments in the garden."

The girls smiled lazily. They seemed somehow to have entered into a land of unrealities and dream pictures. The bamboo and rice paper villa was a doll's house, the lovely garden, a stage setting and the picturesque band of Japanese servants gliding noiselessly about, the chorus.

And while they talked and sipped their tea, a fat, decrepit pug dog came slowly toward them down the walk on spindle legs. As the aged creature approached, O'Haru paused and made it a profound bow. The girls choked and sputtered in their tea and Miss Campbell laughed outright. They learned afterwards that this venerable animal was "Nedda," the Spears' pet pug, eighteen years old, and that every servant attached to the household regarded her with great respect because they believed that she was really Mr. Spears' grandmother.

Old Nedda was very pleased to meet with a little human company of her own social status. She wagged her twisted tail cordially and when she heard American voices speaking the language of her youth, she gave a little expressive whine of pleasure.

"You poor old lonesome thing," exclaimed the compassionate Billie.

Just then a maid hurried up with a cushion. She had evidently been detailed to look after Nedda in the absence of the mistress of the house; to feed and bathe her; to see that she was covered up at night; to guard against her sleeping in damp places. Nedda stepped gingerly on the mat, moved round and round in a circle several times, even as the most primitive dog might do, and settled herself in a round heap for her late afternoon siesta. Then O'Sudzu, the little maid, spread a wadded silk cover over the pampered old Nedda and departed, bowing again.

They were still laughing over this absurd incident when Mr. Campbell appeared on the walk with two companions. One was a good looking young man about twenty-one and the other a Japanese in European clothes, and very handsome, the girls thought him, in spite of his Oriental features and dark complexion.

CHAPTER II.

TEA IN THE GARDEN.

Nancy Brown instinctively put her hand to her curls when she saw the three approach. Elinor patted her coronet braids. Mary blushed and shrank timidly into the depths of her chair, for she was very shy; and Billie, whose candid nature had no coquetry, looked calmly interested and remarked:

"Dear old Papa, there he is with two visitors."

"I'm not at all surprised," said Miss Campbell smiling, "your Papa is one of the most general inviters I ever knew. He always loved to entertain."

"How do my five beautiful American ladies feel?" called her jovial relation as he entered the summer house. "Rested with humble refreshment in poor modest little house?"

"Yes, indeed, honorable father," answered Billie laughing.

"I want you to meet my two friends, Nicholas Grimm and Yoritomo Ito," went on Mr. Campbell.

Nicholas Grimm was apparently a young Dutchman. His figure was well set up and stocky, his features regular, his mouth firm with a good square chin, and his clear dark eyes under bushy brows gazed on the world with a frank, good-humored expression.

Yoritomo I to was the best type of Japanese, lithe and straight,

　　　　　　　　　KATHERINE STOKES

rather tall, with shrewd brown eyes and a smile that always hovered about his shapely mouth. He was immaculately neat and his skin looked as if it might have been scrubbed and then polished. Not a speck of dust marred his spotless linen or his dark blue suit.

"Mr. Ito, will you sit on a mat on the floor or in a chair?" asked Miss Campbell when the introductions were over.

"Oh, he can be Japanese or American, whichever suits him," interrupted Mr. Campbell, "though I'll wager you didn't do much floor sitting when you went to Harvard, did you, Yoritomo?"

The Japanese's smile broadened somewhat when he answered with a slight accent:

"American floors are not intended to be used as chairs."

"Meaning, Mr. Ito, that the American floors are not as entirely free from dust as the Japanese floors?" inquired Miss Campbell.

"Oh, no, Madam," protested the Japanese, horrified at this implication of rudeness but unable to dispel the impression nevertheless.

"I grant you that our houses are not as clean as yours," went on Miss Campbell, "but you see we haven't time to remove our shoes whenever we enter the house, and then we have so much furniture and so many hangings to catch the dust. I don't see how you Japanese can resist the collecting habit in a country where there are so many beautiful things to collect."

"My dear Cousin, they are as great collectors as anybody, only they keep their valuables stored in a fire-proof house - what is it you call it, Yoritomo?" asked Mr. Campbell.

"It is called in English language a 'go-down.'"

"So it is, a 'go-down.' It always reminds me of a steep grade down the side of a mountain. Here they keep all their best clothes and vases and ornaments and only bring out one vase and one scroll at a time. When they grow tired of those things, they are stored and something else is brought out, so that there is perpetual variety in the Japanese home."

"I should hate to have my best clothes locked in a fire-proof house," announced Nancy. "Suppose one wanted to make a quick change and the key was mislaid."

"Ah, Miss Nancy," laughed Mr. Campbell, "it is not difficult to see where your heart lies."

Yoritomo looked at Nancy with polite though evident interest which gradually developed into a cautiously veiled admiration. He was about to speak, when he was interrupted by the troop of little maids headed by Onoye with tea and refreshments. It was Onoye who served the young Japanese. First she bowed before him until her forehead almost touched the ground. Then she placed a mat for him to sit upon and a low lacquer tray containing tea and rice cakes. But Yoritomo, ignoring these humble services, sat himself in a chair next to Nancy and little Onoye hastened to rectify her mistake.

In the meantime, Nicholas Grimm was talking to Billie and Elinor.

"Are you from Holland?" they asked him.

"Several hundreds of years ago I was. Kinterhook, New York, has been my home for the last generation."

"Good," exclaimed Billie, "I thought you were a Dutchman and it's lots nicer to be an American, don't you think so?"

"I wouldn't care to change," answered Nicholas solemnly. "America's good enough for me."

KATHERINE STOKES

"Are you one of the engineers on the new railroad they are building?" asked Billie.

"I'm going to lay a few ties," he answered.

"Are you going to build those little funny openwork bridges over all the streams?" demanded Elinor.

"Something like it. Everything is picturesque in this country from beggars to railroad bridges, and, speaking of bridges, have you explored the garden yet? There's a ripping little bridge down there. When Mrs. Spears gave garden parties that was one of the strolling places."

"Why, we didn't know we had such a pretentious garden!" exclaimed Billie. "Papa wrote that he had sublet a suburban villa near Tokyo with an acre or so of ground around it."

"An acre or so?" repeated Nicholas. "That's an estate to them. They can put as much into an acre without crowding it as other people put into ten. Perhaps you would like to explore the garden if you have had enough honorable refreshment?"

"Oh, yes," they answered eagerly, and drawing shy little Mary from the depths of her chair, Billie followed Elinor and the new friend down the garden path.

"Would you be interested in seeing the garden?" asked Yoritomo of Nancy.

"I might be induced," she answered drooping her long eyelashes, to the great amusement of Mr. Campbell, and they also wandered off, leaving the two older people for a cousinly chat.

The girls were amazed at the beauty of the garden back of the house. Against the high wall surrounding the small estate clustered masses of flowers. Everywhere were little winding paths and an occasional grove of stunted pines that gave the impression of great age. It was in exquisite order, the green turf clipped to the smoothness of a velvet carpet. In all the garden there was not a leaf nor twig out of place. Back of the house the land sloped slightly and at the foot of this gentle depression trickled a musical little stream. Here was a stone lantern five feet high, also the miniature curved bridge; and to make the picture complete in every Japanese detail, leaning pensively on the railing of the bridge, stood Onoye. She herself might have been a bright colored flower in her gay kimono and sash.

Only Mary noticed that the little Japanese was weeping softly. When she saw the Americans coming, she hastily withdrew down one of the paths and in another moment had disappeared entirely.

"Poor little thing," thought Mary, "perhaps her mother has been scolding her."

Perhaps she had, indeed, for O'Haru, the housekeeper, presently appeared looking for her daughter. Shading her eyes with one hand, she scanned the vistas of the garden.

Mary left the group of friends and hastened down the path.

"Are you looking for Onoye?" she asked the old woman.

"Yes, honorable lady," answered O'Haru, trying to replace her uneasy and troubled expression with a pleasant smile.

"She was on the bridge a moment ago. Is she unhappy? I think she was crying."

"Have greatly kindness to forgive humble Japanese girl," answered O'Haru in a low voice.

Mary thought the housekeeper was going to say more and no doubt, if she had poured out her confidences at that time, many later misunderstandings might have been averted. As it was, they were interrupted by Nancy and her Japanese cavalier who turned the curve of the path and came full upon them quite suddenly.

Instead of hastening away as quietly as possible, O'Haru immediately fell on her knees and began speaking in a low voice in her own language.

There was nothing unusual in this. All the servants seemed to be in a continual state of "nervous prostration," as Billie expressed it, and Nancy, smiling and dimpling, followed Yoritomo down the path without thinking any more about O'Haru.

"What was she saying, Mr. Ito?" she asked.

"You might accuse me of being a flatterer if I told you," he answered.

"But I don't understand."

"I mean she was speaking of you. 'The honorable young American lady,'" she said, "'is very beautiful.'"

Nancy was flattered, as who would not have been over this frank compliment. A rosy flush spread over her face and the dimple deepened in her cheek.

"You see, you are an unusual type in this country, Miss Brown," continued the Japanese. "You must expect to arouse comment wherever you go. Hair with so much color to it, like polished copper and curling, too, causes much admiration. You are very different from the Japanese."

Again Nancy felt flattered.

"I really believe I am rather pretty," she thought. What she said was: "You are very kind, Mr. Ito, but I am sure I think the Japanese girls are just as pretty as American girls. Little Onoye, our maid, is charming. She is a perfect picture."

For the rest of the day, however, vain Nancy was enveloped in a rosy cloud of self-satisfaction. It was pleasing to be admired and still more pleasing to feel that the admiration was justified.

The truth is, that admiration was quite as stimulating to Nancy as it is to the rest of us, and when she realized that the young Japanese had fallen an instant victim to her charms, she felt some pardonable pride in the power of her blue eyes and bright curls.

By this time the others had returned to the pagoda-like summer house.

"Come, Nancy, dear," floated Miss Campbell's voice across the garden. She was too careful a chaperone to permit one of her girls to wander at dusk with a strange young Japanese.

Nancy quickened her pace. Nevertheless, she felt a little impatient with all these restrictions.

"I am almost eighteen. I suppose I might be trusted to look after myself occasionally," she thought with some irritation.

"May I not see you again to-morrow, Miss Brown?" Yoritomo was asking.

"I am afraid you'll have to ask Miss Campbell."

"It is now almost the American dinner hour," he went on thoughtfully, looking at his watch. "If I should be strolling to-morrow at this time down by the bridge, it would be very pleasant. We could have a few words together."

"But -" began Nancy, and the voices of her friends interrupted her.

They had paused near a great bush of azaleas in full bloom.

KATHERINE STOKES

Almost over their heads the silver crescent of the new moon hung poised like a fairy scimitar. It was exquisite and unreal. Nancy felt somehow out of place in the lovely picture, while the young Japanese, standing intense and rigid beside her, was as much a part of the Oriental garden as the stone lantern and the fragrant spice bush near the path. Even his blue serge European suit seemed to have lost its values in the deepening shadows.

"If I come every day to see you, there would be great comment," he said in a low voice. "But often I shall wait on the bridge about this time."

It was only a little time ago that Nancy's mother had lengthened her little daughter's skirts from shoe tops to ankles. The line of the old hem was still noticeable in some of her summer frocks. Just six months since, Nancy had tucked up the bunch of curls into a Psyche knot and transformed the ribbon bow into a velvet bandeau. Since she had been old enough to go to parties she had had boy admirers who had said sweet things to her. But this was quite different, and Nancy, almost eighteen, and capable of looking after herself, felt suddenly frightened.

"I - I must hurry," she said, and turning she ran as fast as she could up the garden path nearly colliding with Billie and Mary who had come to look for her.

"Why, Nancy, you are chasing along like a scared rabbit," cried Billie. "Has anything happened to you?"

"Oh, no. I thought we had better run because it was so late," she answered breathlessly, while Yoritomo, following close behind, calm and collected, bade them a formal good night and hurried over to the summer house to pay his respects to Miss Campbell and her cousin.

Nancy decided that night not to tell Billie, her intimate confidante, what the Japanese had said to her. The walls were too thin, she thought. Besides, she was curious to know if Yoritomo would be on the bridge the next afternoon. Just how she intended to find this out, she had not then decided.

CHAPTER III.

SHOPPING IN JINRIKSHAS.

"I feel very much like a baby in a baby carriage," observed Miss Helen Campbell as Mr. Campbell almost lifted her into the graceful little two-wheeled vehicle. "And is that poor soul going to turn into a horse and pull me?" she demanded.

"You aren't such a heavy load," replied her cousin. "I doubt if the S. P. C. A. would get excited over it. I am only sorry you have to be alone, but I suppose those four inseparables are paired off as usual. Billie with Nancy and Mary with Elinor."

"Indeed, I much prefer to be alone," said Miss Campbell. "Then I can hold on with both hands in case I am upset backwards."

"You never will be. They will treat you like spun glass. You will take good care of the ladies, Komatsu," he said to the 'riksha man who, leaning against the garden wall, resembled a bronze figure, brown and muscular.

"Gracious lady of fearing not need," answered Komatsu with an ingratiating smile as he stepped between the shafts of the 'riksha.

"It is impossible to tell how much English they know and how much they don't know," Mr. Campbell confided to his relative in a low voice. "They never ask twice and they always make some kind of an out at a reply. But I think, until I can go with you, it is safer for you to go in the 'rikshas. The common people here aren't used to motor cars and there are still some fanatics in Japan, you know, who are opposed to every sort of progress and the invasion of foreign customs."

"Good-by, Papa," called Billie, "I do wish you were not a working man so that you could go with us."

"I am sorry I must be a laborer in the vineyards, Miss Wilhelmina," he answered, "but it's only that you may ride in a fine carriage and wear a silk robe."

"Silk robe?" repeated Miss Campbell. "That's just what I want. Komatsu, we wish to go to a silk shop," she ordered the man-servant, speaking very loud and distinctly as if she were addressing a deaf person.

Komatsu grinned amiably.

"I bring honorable lady to fine shop with quickness."

The next moment the three vehicles were flying along the road drawn by three tireless individuals, whose good nature, like the widow's cruse, knew no diminishing.

It would be difficult to find in all the world a more beautiful city than Tokyo at this season of the year. It is really a city of gardens and everywhere are palms and pines and waving willow trees, magnificent arbors of wisteria not yet in bloom and splendid azalea bushes bursting into masses of white and pink blossoms. Even the humblest brown cottage has its bit of garden, for the love of flowers is innate in every Japanese nature: it is a national trait.

"There is no prospect that isn't graceful and picturesque," thought Mary watching an old fruit and vegetable man in front of them. He wore a dull blue cotton tunic much faded but still a heavenly color, and on either end of a pole resting on his shoulders was a flat brown basket filled with small oranges and vegetables of an unknown variety. Behind him walked an old woman in a dull brown and purple dress with an orange sash around her waist. Her back was burdened with a great bundle of bark. The sun was hot and many of the wayfarers carried paper umbrellas. Most of the women had babies swung on their backs and sometimes shiny little black eyes peeped out from the front of a kimono, the mother's arms being engaged in supporting another burden on her back.

"It seems to me the women work very hard in this country," remarked Elinor severely, pointing to a cart filled with charcoal propelled by two women and a man. One of the women had a baby on her back and another child holding to her skirts.

"They do," said Mary. "Even the women in the upper classes have to work hard. Don't you remember what the missionary on the steamer told us? The wife is always the first one up in the household no matter how many servants she has. She has to bring her mean old mother-in-law a cup of tea and get out her husband's clothes. The mother-in-law has had to work so hard when she was a daughter-in-law that she takes it out on her son's wife later."

"I'd like to see an American wife ridden by her mother-in-law that way," broke in Elinor indignantly.

"But then the Japanese daughter-in-law's turn comes later," said Mary laughing, "when she gets to be a mother-in-law. So it's all nicely balanced."

But the streets were too interesting to pursue the subject of mother-in-law any further. They were passing a row of open-fronted shops on the edges of which customers were squatted looking at materials while the proprietor bobbed and smiled and dickered over his bargains. Red and yellow banners hung in a row from the roof of the shop, the gay colored hieroglyphics on them indicating what manner of goods were displayed within.

"Here's a nice little silk shop, Komatsu. Let us stop here," called Miss Campbell.

But Komatsu only grinned over his shoulder and called:

"Too littleness for gracious big lady."

"But I like the looks of this place, Komatsu," said the gracious big lady helplessly.

However Komatsu had his own ideas of obedience and he trotted on, never pausing until he reached a large silk store thronged with clerks and customers.

Here all the 'rikshas drew up and the girls alighted with Miss Campbell, who was a little red in the face but determined to overlook the annoyance of orders disregarded.

The front of the store was screened from the street by dark blue cotton curtains behind which was a roofed platform carpeted with matting. Here sat a group of clerks, each with his *soroban* or adding machine at his side. Little Japanese boys, their shoulders loaded with bales of rich materials, staggered about, and through the open doors of the fire-proof warehouse they caught glimpses of costly stuffs stored away. An obsequious clerk who spoke excellent English came forward and presently, when their eyes became accustomed to the busy, brilliantly colored scene, they began to examine silk materials on their own account. Miss Campbell made each of her charges a present of *crêpe de chine* and still was not very much out of pocket. As they were about to leave, they were followed by a chorus of shouts.

"What in the world is the matter?" demanded Miss Campbell uneasily. "Has the place caught fire, or didn't we give the right amount of change?"

"No, madam," answered the polite English-speaking clerk, who had accompanied her to the sidewalk. "They are saying farewell. In English it would mean, 'Thanks for your continued favors.'"

"Don't mention it," said Miss Campbell. "We'll come again."

The clerk smiled and bowed formally and once more they whirled away in their 'rikshas. They visited many shops in Tokyo that morning. It was like a fascinating bazaar and it seemed impossible to tear themselves away, although Komatsu kept always close to their elbows and several times observed:

"Muchly more time. Come again."

At last, just as an ominous mass of black clouds had spread itself over the heavens, against which the brilliant colors of the signs and the people's clothes stood out in bold relief, they started for home. But on the outskirts of the city great drops of rain pelted them in the face, the advance scouts of a tremendous downpour.

"Oh, Komatsu, we will ruin our clothes," cried Miss Campbell in alarm. "You must take us somewhere until the rain is over."

They were passing the high walls of a garden, the gate of which stood open. Without an instant's hesitation Komatsu turned in and the three 'rikshas raced up a broad walk toward a Japanese house at the end. Several smiling hospitable persons whom they took to be servants ran out with large umbrellas made of oiled paper and protected the five ladies, who hurried unceremoniously into the house just as the heavens opened and the rain came down in bucketfuls.

Three Japanese ladies, seated on the floor drinking tea, rose quickly and made low formal bows. The five refugees from the storm returned the bows with some bewilderment.

"I do hope you will pardon this intrusion," Miss Campbell found herself saying. "The storm was so sudden and terrible, we fled to the nearest house."

One of the little Japanese ladies bowed. She was evidently the mistress of the house, but she spoke no English.

Miss Campbell pointed outside to the rain and made expressive signs indicative of haste. It was really like being in a deaf and dumb asylum. Then the little lady smiled again and bowed again, and the others bowed.

"Good heavens, Billie, what am I to do? Must I continue to smile and bob and bow forever? Do come to my rescue!"

But the hospitable hostess now hurried from the room and presently reappeared followed by her maids, each of whom carried a little lacquered table. It was indicated that the American guests would confer a favor if they would seat themselves.

"I've never sat on the floor in my life," complained Miss Campbell in a low voice. "It will kill me. I am certain it will displace a ligament."

"You'll just have to, Cousin. Try sitting on your feet. That's the way they do."

"I think tailor-fashion would be easier," answered the poor lady. "Don't help me. They might take it for rudeness. Everything is bad manners in this country."

Crossing her feet, she slid slowly to the floor. The visitors were promptly served with delicious tea, rice cakes, candied fruits and other confections molded and colored like the flowers in season.

Certainly that was one of the most silent and ceremonious tea parties ever given. It was all dumb show, but the manners of the three Japanese ladies were exquisite. While this excruciatingly polite scene transpired, there raged such a storm of wind and rain that at each moment they feared the fragile bamboo and rice paper abode would be blown from its slight foundations.

"They won't lose much if it's blown away," thought Billie. "There's not a stick of furniture to be seen except a screen."

In one corner of the room was a splendid vase almost as tall as she was, and on the wall hung a scroll showing two women gathering cherry blossoms. On the floor were soft mats fitted closely together.

Suddenly Billie blushed scarlet.

"Oh, Cousin Helen," she exclaimed. "We forgot to take off our shoes."

"Don't speak to me," answered her relation. "My legs have gone to sleep and I have lost the power to move them. I am in an agony of pain."

At this moment a figure darkened the doorway. The three Japanese women rose and bowed low and the servants made obeisances. The five Americans were amazed to recognize their friend of yesterday, Yoritomo Ito. He was quite as amazed as they were, although he did not show it except by the flick of an eyelash, because no well-bred Japanese ever shows surprise.

"How do you do, Mr. Ito?" cried Miss Campbell. "Is it possible that this is your house we have broken into so rudely?"

It was indeed Mr. Ito's home, and, the three ladies were his mother, his aunt and his sister.

"It is a great pleasure, I am sure, that you have found refuge in my home. I trust they have served you well."

Then he spoke rapidly in Japanese to his mother, who smiled and clasped her hands with joy, as if heaven could not have bestowed a greater gift than the privilege to entertain these delightful foreigners.

"And are you the head of the family, Mr. Ito?" asked Miss Campbell.

"No, my father takes first place. He is a tea merchant in Tokyo. I have also a younger brother who works with him. He did not wish to go to America with me."

At this moment a human doll baby toddled into the room. His round little head was bald except for a thick mat of hair on top. His beady black eyes gleamed like polished glass. He wore a dark red kimono and his feet and legs were bare.

"Oh, the darling," cried Mary whose love of children overcame any shyness she might feel before strangers. The three Japanese were pleased at the attention the little person created. The girls gathered around him in a circle while he stood perfectly still regarding them curiously, as if they were some new strange birds which had dropped into his room from the skies.

Yoritomo also was pleased. He took the little fellow's hand in his and led him from one to another while his relatives stood in a beaming row.

Children are called "treasure-flowers" in Japan, and are petted and spoiled quite as much as American children.

"What a cunning little baby brother, Mr. Ito," said Nancy. "What is his name?"

"Kenkyo," answered Yoritomo. Suddenly he turned and spoke to one of the women and the "treasure-flower" was led from the room.

"Oh, don't send him away," objected Miss Campbell. "I haven't had half a chance to see him yet."

"He is not dressed to see distinguished visitors," answered Yoritomo, quickly. "My mother would like to show you some of her embroidery if you would care to see it."

So the subject of little Kenkyo was dropped and Madame Ito, hurrying away, returned in a moment with an armful of linen and silk on which she had worked the most wonderful floral designs.

In the meantime, the faithful 'riksha man, Komatsu, had trotted all the way through floods of rain to the Campbell villa half a mile distant, and now returned in company with O'Haru. Between them they carried a covered basket containing five mackintoshes, five pairs of overshoes and five umbrellas.

Komatsu was very angry with O'Haru. He explained to Miss Campbell:

"I not wish, but she coming without not wish."

He pointed accusingly at the sad old face. O'Haru, dripping and imperturbable, stood on the piazza near the entrance to the villa.

"That was very good of you, O'Haru; we appreciate your devotion," said Miss Campbell, but the housekeeper did not appear to grasp all this fine English. She seemed to be taking in every detail of the room and its occupants. Nobody took any notice of her. All the ladies and the servants were engaged in helping the guests on with their rain coats and overshoes. Mme. Ito insisted on doing up their hats in paper bundles.

In the midst of a great deal of leave-taking and much smiling and bowing, Yoritomo found time to say to Nancy:

"You see, chance has favored me to-day. The rain which kept me away from the bridge has brought you to my home."

Nancy blushed in spite of her efforts not to. She felt half pleased and half frightened at the earnest manner of the young Japanese. He was undeniably handsome and graceful, with a self-possession she had never seen equaled. Just then a dark figure darted across the floor so swiftly that it was like a flash of brown wings in the air. There was a low exclamation from the ladies, a bird-like chatter from the servants, and for one brief moment the surprised Americans beheld old O'Haru on her knees before little Kenkyo in the act of touching her forehead to the floor. She drew a beautiful, bright-colored toy from her bosom and gave it to the solemn-eyed little boy. Then, bowing again with extreme reverence, she rose and left the house. When they next saw her she was swinging along in the rain on her wooden clogs. Miss Campbell made Komatsu stop the 'riksha and invited her to climb in, but she refused politely but firmly.

"Extraordinary creature," exclaimed Miss Campbell, but Komatsu could offer no explanation.

KATHERINE STOKES

CHAPTER IV.

THE GARDEN IN THE RAIN.

For three interminable days the rain poured down uninterruptedly. The floodgates of heaven had opened and it seemed as though they would never close again. The all-pervading dampness and chill brought illness to the Campbell household of a kind not to be healed by medicine. Homesickness it was, and it spread rapidly like a contagious disease. Only one member of the party of Americans was not afflicted and that was Mr. Campbell, who had lived in many climates and countries and was accustomed to seasons of rain and wet. Moreover, as he himself had said, he had no home to be sick for. He felt a supreme content in the thought of having his daughter with him and no amount of rain could chill his enthusiasm.

Miss Campbell took to her bed with an attack of rheumatism, brought on, she insisted, from having sat on the floor at the home of Mme. Ito. Mary began a diary of her experiences in Japan and had several private weeping spells entirely due to the unsurpassed dismalness of the weather. Billie endeavored to throw off her depression by giving Onoye lessons in English in exchange for lessons in Japanese, and in the course of these lessons she learned a little of Onoye's history. O'Haru had been obliged to go to work after the death of her husband who had lost all his property in a fire. Onoye's only brother had been killed in great "bat-tel." The family had had "muchly unfortune. All money gone - nothing."

At the conclusion of this sad story told mostly by expressive gestures and queerly chosen words, Onoye smiled sweetly. That is the only polite thing for a well brought up Japanese girl to do even when her own misfortunes are the subject of the conversation.

"What a shame," Billie exclaimed sympathetically. "I should think you would learn something, some trade, I mean, Onoye. You are much too clever to be a housemaid. But I suppose you will marry. I hear there are no old maids in Japan."

Onoye shook her head and smiled sadly. Perhaps she did not understand Billie's remark because she did not reply.

"Old maid, Onoye, is one who never marries," explained Nancy at the dressing table arranging her hair.

"Ah, Komatsu old maid. He not marry."

"No, no, Komatsu is a man," said Billie trying not to laugh. "Old maid is a woman who has no husband, like Miss Campbell."

"Old maid," repeated Onoye, and because of what happened that very evening, it was evident that the retentive Japanese memory had not lost the words.

In the afternoon there came a characteristic note from Mr. Campbell to his cousin.

"Tell O'Haru to put on the big pot and the little," it ran, "and to kill the fatted calf. I am going to cheer up my gloomy household by bringing four men home to dinner. If it were not for these flimsy little card houses, I would suggest a dance afterwards, but I couldn't answer for the walls and roof if two young Americans danced a two-step in the parlor."

"I am sure a two-step is no rougher than one of these storms of wind and rain," observed Miss Campbell, feeling a sudden loyalty toward everything American, including dances.

O'Haru was informed of the party and the house became at once a beehive of activity. Several of the little maids, without being told, took down all the dresses in the wardrobes and began drying them out with square boxes of red embers.

"I'd like to be done the same way," remarked Miss Campbell. "I think I am just as mildewed as my clothes."

The kitchen quarters of the house fairly vibrated with the stir of preparation. In the living rooms the air was dried with small charcoal stoves. The gardener was seen bringing in armfuls of flowers; and with all the activity and preparation, there was no noise, not a sound. It was positively uncanny.

Late in the afternoon Nancy slipped away from this noiseless busy scene and tripped demurely down a garden path toward the bridge. She was not exactly bent on mischief but she wanted to satisfy her curiosity about something. The rain had lessened considerably but it was still necessary for her to protect her recently arranged curls with her small blue silk umbrella. In her mackintosh of changeable silk in two shades of blue, she made a charming picture coming down the rain-soaked path. The garden itself was a thing of beauty. On the end of every pine needle hung a crystal drop, and through the thin veil of mist clinging to the shrubbery a clump of azaleas glowed like a crimson flame. Taking a path to the left, Nancy began the gentle and almost imperceptible descent to the little bridge. The air was filled with the perfume of wild roses and late plum blossoms. It was really a fairy land, this Japan; a place too exquisite and unreal for human beings to live in. She began to sing softly to herself Elinor's favorite song:

"'Know'st thou the land of the citron bloom?'"

As she approached the bridge she felt a little frightened for some reason. It was rather reckless of her to come down to this lonely place in the late afternoon even if it was their own premises. It was the first time she had done it and she decided it would be the last. But as long as she had come, she would see it through. Nancy could hardly explain to herself what she meant by "seeing it through."

She would stroll carelessly down the path, walk across the bridge, pause a moment and walk back again, not looking behind her of course, as, if she were observed, and she was sure she was not, she would pretend she was out for a walk and had not expected to meet anyone. Thus Nancy reasoned with herself, but by the time she had reached the bridge she had changed her mind and was about to turn and hasten back, when she noticed a beautiful tea rose that had been laid conspicuously on the hand rail of the bridge.

"He has been here," she thought. "He must have just gone. The rose is quite fresh."

Sticking its long stem through the buttonhole of her raincoat, she glanced about her curiously. Somehow, behind every clump of shrubs and every branching pine tree she felt black eyes staring at her and yet she was sure she was alone. Again she started for the house, feeling profoundly relieved that Yoritomo had not waited, if, indeed, it was he who had left the rose. Suddenly Nancy's heart jumped into her throat and she felt a cold chill down her spinal column, - and for no reason, except that standing in front of her was not a man, but a woman. The stranger was too tall to be a Japanese and she was dressed, moreover, in European clothes, - a beautifully fitting tailor-made suit and English traveling hat of stitched cloth. But there was something faintly suggestive of the Japanese about her face. Perhaps it was the slightly slanting eyes and the smooth olive skin. Her hair was much lighter than her eyes and quite fluffy; her features were regular and there was a graceful dignity in the poise of her head on her shoulders. Nancy concluded after a swift examination that she was, if peculiar looking, still strangely fascinating.

"May I ask your pardon for intruding on your beautiful gardens?" began the woman, speaking with a slightly English accent. "I did not expect to meet any one on this rainy afternoon."

Nancy wondered how she had got into the garden and where she had come from. These things the stranger did not explain. However, Nancy answered politely:

"It isn't my garden, but I am sure Mr. Campbell would be delighted to have other people enjoy it."

"You are a sweet child," said the woman, deliberately taking Nancy's chin in her hand and looking down at her, "a sweet, exquisite child."

After all, Nancy decided, this mysterious lady was both fascinating and beautiful.

"And who is Mr. Campbell?"

Nancy explained. In fact, after a few leading questions, she disclosed the entire history of the household; who they were, how long they expected to stay, and how they happened to be spending the summer in Japan.

"Is it possible that you are the Motor Maids who have ridden so many thousands of miles in a red car?" asked the stranger.

Nancy opened her eyes.

"Yes," she answered. "But we never dreamed we were so famous as that."

"Ah, you will find that Tokyo is not so far removed from the world," answered the woman, smiling gravely. "And Mr. Campbell is building a railroad, you say?"

"No, I didn't say so," replied Nancy, a little surprised. "He's not building anything that I know of. He is being consulted, or something."

But the stranger did not seem to have heard her.

"I must be going," she said absently. "You are an adorably pretty child. It's been a pleasure to see you. I only wandered in here because I was unhappy and wanted to be alone, but you have cheered me up. Run along, now, and don't walk in Japanese gardens at dusk unattended too often." Her glance fell on the tea rose. "And remember that the Japanese do not understand the meaning of the word 'flirtation.' Good-by, *ma cherie, belle et charmante.* You won't tell your Mr. Campbell that I trespassed on his garden, will you? Promise?"

"I promise," answered Nancy, quite bewildered and fascinated.

Then the mysterious lady disappeared down a dripping path and Nancy was left standing alone in the rain.

"I am sorry I promised," was her first thought. "It would have been such fun to tell Billie." But her second thought was: "Billie would have asked me why I had gone walking at dusk in the rain, and what a teasing I should have got."

It was late and she hurried back to dress for dinner. No one had missed her because Billie had been helping Miss Campbell into her best evening frock, and the others were all engaged in their own toilets.

That evening at half past seven a very jolly party gathered around the dinner table, which was a miracle of beauty with its decorations of apple blossoms. Besides Nicholas Grimm and Yoritomo Ito, there were two Englishmen, Reginald Carlton, a young man who was taking a trip around the world by way of finishing his education, and Mr. Buxton, an older man who lived in Tokyo. All the men wore evening clothes, although Mr. Campbell had sighed when Billie made him appear in his. He was a man of camps and open air and seldom appeared in society. Nancy watched his rugged, handsome face admiringly.

"What a splendid looking man he is," she was thinking, when

Yoritomo at her right said in a low voice:

"You did go to the bridge."

"How do you know?" she asked.

"Because I saw the rose. It was fastened on your rain coat, which you left on a hook in the passage with your wet umbrella."

"I only went for the air," said Nancy hastily. "I shall not go again alone."

Yoritomo's face darkened, and he turned his attention to his dinner.

In the meantime the others were all amusing themselves in various ways, and there was a great deal of talk and laughter. Miss Campbell felt rejuvenated and her rheumatic twinges had entirely disappeared.

"There is nothing like a little pleasure for driving acidity out of the system," she thought, as she finished the last spoonful of her dessert of beautifully preserved fruits.

Onoye had entered, carrying a small lacquered tray on which lay a square, foreign-looking visiting card.

"A lady calling to the honorable old maid," she announced calmly at Miss Campbell's elbow.

"The what?" cried Mr. Campbell.

"The honorable old maid," repeated poor Onoye, with her precise accent, smiling innocently.

There was a perfect shout of laughter. Only Yoritomo's face remained impassive, but who could tell what angry thoughts were hidden behind that mask-like face? Billie tried to explain how the mistake had occurred, and Onoye rushed from the room in an agony of embarrassment and shame.

"Don't scold her, Cousin. She thought she had learned a new English word," Billie besought Miss Campbell.

"Scold her? I should think not. I don't mind being called an 'honorable old maid,' I am sure. But who is this caller, I wonder?" she added, in a lower voice.

Mr. Campbell examined the card with some curiosity. "Mme. Marie Fontaine," it read. Miss Campbell hastened into the drawing-room, and Nancy, peeping through the doors a few minutes later, was surprised to find that Mme. Fontame was her recent companion in the garden.

The visit was very brief, and Miss Campbell presently returned looking somewhat amused and a little annoyed.

"Mme. Fontaine wished to know if she might have an interview with the Motor Maids on the subject of their motor trip across the American continent and through the British Isles."

"And what did you tell her?" demanded the four girls in one voice, it must be confessed somewhat eagerly.

"I told her that while we appreciated the compliment, it would be impossible."

"Quite right," said Mr. Campbell. "Publicity is the thing of all others I wish to avoid, and if an article like that appeared in a Tokyo paper, either in Japanese or English, you would probably be the object of the most disagreeable curiosity. Am I not right, Yoritomo?"

"Oh, yes. It would not be agreeable to the young ladies. Many people would come to look at them."

"I am very glad my action is approved, then," said Miss Campbell. "I have an old-fashioned horror of notoriety like that, and I am sure none of my girls would care to see herself in a newspaper. Would she?"

"No, indeed," they answered promptly in a chorus.

In a secret place in Nancy's mind, however, she saw a picture of her own pretty face occupying at least one-third of a newspaper page and underneath, blazoned in large letters: "The Beautiful Miss Anne Starbuck Brown, One of the Famous Motor Maids."

CHAPTER V.

IN THE LIBRARY.

The house Mr. Campbell had sub-let for the summer was somewhat labyrinthian in design, since it was only one story high and contained many rooms for living and sleeping, besides the servants' quarters in the rear. Mr. Spears had engaged a Japanese architect to build the house and Japanese and European ideas were curiously combined in its construction. Down the middle ran a broad hall, intersected at the back by another hall running across the house. This was known as "the passage," and it was in a manner a social boundary line, dividing the quarters of master and servants. Only one opening broke the monotony of the uninterrupted partition on the far side of the passage. This was the door into the library which had been placed in a quiet and out-of-the-way corner overlooking the garden.

This library was decidedly the most attractive and home-like room in the villa. There was a large open fireplace at one end where a pile of blazing logs now crackled cheerfully. It would have taken an immense "go-down" to accommodate all the books which lined the walls. But Mr. Spears was evidently not afraid of fire, for they stood in serried ranks, rows and rows of them, and between each group of shelves was a panel of carved and polished wood. Over the mantel hung a beautiful Japanese print. Curtains of some heavy material, old rose in color, hung at the windows, and instead of the usual three by six mats, the floor was covered with an Oriental rug in soft warm colors. There were many low, comfortable chairs about and several tables on which stood shaded lamps.

Later in the evening after Mr. Campbell's dinner party, the three older members of the company sat down in the drawing-room for a quiet game, while the young people repaired to the library where they might talk and laugh freely without fear of disturbing the players.

"Oh, I say, what a jolly room," exclaimed Reginald Carlton, looking about him with interest.

"Isn't it?" agreed Billie. "Papa says that if people would only stick to Japanese notions of decoration and add a few comfortable chairs to sit in, they would never make any mistakes. You see, there's only one picture in this room, but that's considered very fine. It's by a famous Japanese artist."

"I like that one-picture idea," put in Nicholas Grimm, "especially if it is at a comfortable elevation. Just pull up an easy chair and raise your eyes and you have seen all there is to see. There's a delightful simplicity about that to me. But I suppose Yoritomo would call this room crowded, nevertheless. How about it, old man? It wouldn't take you fifteen minutes to pull down the curtains and roll up the rug and store them in the 'go-down.' Would it, now, honor bright?"

"No, no. I like the European furnishings," protested the Japanese. "You must remember that I lived in America for many years. There is only one thing I would store in the 'go-down,' and that is the little safe."

He pointed to a small American fire-proof safe in a corner of the room.

"But that is our 'go-down,'" laughed Billie. "We haven't any other. When Papa first came here he discovered that there was no place to lock up anything except some desk drawers, and he rented this little safe for his papers. A Japanese gentleman advised him to do it. He told Papa there was a great deal of curiosity here about the private business of foreigners."

A dark flush overspread Yoritomo's face and gradually faded out. The others did not notice it, however. They had followed Nicholas across the room and were standing in a circle around the safe, while the young American touched it with a caressing hand.

"Made in Newark, N.J., U.S.A.," he exclaimed. "Think of that. It's like meeting an old friend from home."

"A very proper kind of friend," observed Reginald. "The kind that keeps a secret behind a combination lock."

"I don't call it being a real friend to have any combination at all," put in Elinor, "because anybody who learns the combination can get the secret."

Nicholas laughed.

"You don't understand the Japanese, Miss Butler," he exclaimed. "They regard all persons with important secrets as combination safes. Sooner or later they believe they can learn any combination if they only persist."

"Why don't you stand up for your country, Mr. Ito?" asked Nancy.

"What Nicholas says is true," answered Yoritomo. "If the secret concerns his country, the Japanese will learn it if he must give up his life. What you call 'spy' in your language should be changed to patriot, or one who risks all for his country. Every Japanese is a spy, because every Japanese will suffer for Japan."

"Perfectly good logic," said Nicholas.

"Are you a spy?" asked Mary, so innocently that even the imperturbable Yoritomo laughed.

"I am, in the sense of being a patriot," he answered. "There is nothing I would not do for Japan."

"Are you a Samurai?" asked Billie, hardly understanding the meaning of the word.

"My grandfather was. There are no real samurai now. Only descendants."

"But what were they?"

Yoritomo's face became strangely animated.

"A samurai was a soldier," he said. "He was brave and feared neither death nor suffering in any form. He carried two swords, a long one for fighting and a short one for defense. The sword was the emblem of the samurai spirit. He took pride in keeping it sharp and bright."

"Aren't some of the descendants of the old warrior samurai rather fanatical?" asked Reginald. "That is, I mean -" he hesitated, seeing a peculiar gleam in Yoritomo's eyes, "aren't some opposed to the entrance of foreigners into Japan, and the invasion of foreign ideas - perhaps that feeling has died out now?"

"The old samurai defended his country against the foreigner and no descendant of a samurai, either now or ever, would endure for a foreigner to learn the secrets of his country. But that is not fanaticism. That is patriotism. He is very jealous of his country's honor, you understand. You will look at the history of other countries. First it is only a few foreigners; then more and more. They slip into the government. They spread their ideas and customs - they get a foot-hold - then - all of a sudden, what is it? Not Japan any longer - but - America - England."

"Oh, come off, Yoritomo," cried Nicholas, laughing. "What in the name of all the powers are you driving at? There are about forty millions of people on this island and I guess a few foreigners won't make much headway in such a bunch as that."

"At least, you are not afraid of being Americanized, Mr. Ito," broke in Nancy, "since you were educated in America."

"I am not afraid of the invasion of beautiful American young ladies," answered Yoritomo gallantly, and the others laughed and felt somewhat relieved that the conversation had drifted into a less serious vein. They drew their chairs into a circle about the fire and talked pleasantly for some time, when they were summoned back to the drawing-room by Mr. Campbell, who reminded Elinor of a promise she had made to him to sing for them with her guitar.

This performance was a subject of wondering curiosity to the servants of the household. Through the door to the dining-room Elinor caught a glimpse of a multitude of natives crouched on the floor behind the screen, including Komatsu and O'Haru, all the little maids, the numerous grandmothers, and the 'riksha men who had brought the guests out from Tokyo. If the music seemed strange to the Japanese ear trained for centuries to a curious uneven scale, at least they admired Elinor's lovely voice, clear and sweet as a bell. She had a large repertoire and knew all the favorites of everybody. While she was singing "Oh, that we two were Maying," at the request of Miss Campbell, Nancy, seated on the couch beside Billie, near the door, whispered into her friend's ear:

"I left my handkerchief in the library," and slipped into the hall. Hardly a moment later Billie, glancing through the door, saw Nancy in the distance, beckoning violently. She rose and followed, much against her will, thinking perhaps Nancy wished to bestow a confidence which might just as well be kept until later.

"What on earth do you want?" she asked, with the irritability intimate friends use toward each other without meaning really to be cross.

"The queerest thing has happened. The library is perfectly black dark."

"I don't think there is anything specially remarkable about that. The fire had burned low before we left and I suppose one of the maids put out the lamps. The Japs are nothing if not economical."

"They are nothing if not polite, too," argued Nancy. "And I am sure they wouldn't put out the lights before the company left. Besides, they are all listening to Elinor sing."

"Well, the lights are out and I don't see that it matters much, Nancy-Bell. Let's go back and hear the rest of the song."

"Won't you come with me first to get my handkerchief?" pleaded Nancy. "I know exactly where I left it, and I am afraid to go alone, if you want to know the real truth."

"Oh, you little coward," laughed Billie good-naturedly, taking her arm. "Come along, then."

The two young girls hastened down the long hall until they reached the passage.

"Billie," whispered Nancy, pausing at the door. "You won't think me silly if I tell you this? Of course it may have been imagination, but I was awfully frightened when I came in here just now. I opened the door suddenly and ran into the room before I realized it was dark. Then, of course, I stopped short. The door had closed behind me and it seemed to me that some one else was in the room. I remembered that as I opened the door I heard some one move or collide with a chair. I stood perfectly still for an instant. I was really frightened. Then I just flew."

"Perhaps it was one of the servants who had put out the lights and was afraid to acknowledge it," suggested Billie. "The little maids are as timid as wild things."

"But every servant in the house is in the dining room, I tell you. I saw them as I went down the hall, and I counted them just for fun. There were the four little maids and Onoye and O'Haru and Komatsu and the three jinriksha men and the three old grandmothers and the gardener. There aren't any others."

The door leading into the library was not a sliding panel of thick opaquepaper, like the usual Japanese door, but a real European door of heavy wood with a brass handle.

"Don't you think we had better get your father, Billie, or one of the boys?" whispered Nancy, placing a detaining hand on her friend's arm.

"But that would be a needless alarm. Everybody would want to know what was the matter. There would have to be explanations and Cousin Helen would be frightened. Besides, I am sure it was just your vivid imagination, Nancy."

She opened the door very softly and peeped in. The room was flooded with the radiance of two shaded lamps, both burning brightly; in fact, one had been turned up too high, as if lighted in haste.

"Oh," gasped Nancy, in amazement.

But Billie was determined not to be surprised.

"Take my word for it, Nancy; one of the servants put out the lights by mistake, thinking we had finished in here for the night, and when you returned he or she was frightened and lit them again, thinking that honorable American young lady might be displeased."

Nancy found her handkerchief.

"Very well," she said. "If that is your expert opinion I am willing to abide by it, but I was fright -"

Before she could finish one of the long French windows blew open and a gust of wet wind extinguished the lamp on a table near the window. Billie marched boldly over and closed and bolted the window.

"Whoever it was," she said, "must have got out this way."

The girls exchanged a long glance of uneasy speculation. In the dim light of the remaining lamp the room seemed filled with shadows. Billie drew the heavy curtains across the casement. Those at the other window were already drawn.

"Come along, Nancy-Bell," she exclaimed. "Thieves don't blow out lights and then come back and relight them. It would be extremely unprofessional if they did and very reckless besides. It's certain to be one of those timid little persons in a kimono. We had better be getting back to the drawing-room or Papa will be wondering what has become of us."

Hardly had they closed the door after them, when a figure, wrapped from head to foot in a long brown garment something like a cape, emerged from behind the other curtains. Whoever it was, whether man or woman, it was impossible to judge, opened the door, peeped cautiously into the passage and, finding it quite empty, marched boldly out. In another moment the intruder had disappeared into the garden.

As the girls passed along the hall they paused to notice the picturesque group of servants gathered near the door. There was a smile on every face, not a smile of ridicule, but of courteous enjoyment.

"Is there any rude person in the length and breadth of Japan?" thought Billie, while Nancy once more counted heads and then shook her own thoughtfully.

"I don't understand," she pondered, "but Billie is usually right, so I'll just cease to worry."

CHAPTER VI.

CHERRY BLOSSOMS.

A few hours of brilliant sunshine and all the dampness had been sucked up from the earth; the air was warmed and dried and the mists rolled back from the garden, revealing a fairy-land too exquisite to be real.

Something especially wonderful had happened that morning. The faces of the little maids had been filled with a joyous expectancy as they hurried from room to room on their household duties. A mysterious smile hovered on the lips of Komatsu when he appeared to receive his orders. Even old O'Haru was secretly immensely pleased about something, but they all had evidently agreed among themselves to keep the great news secret until the psychological moment had arrived when the ladies of the house and Mr. Campbell had assembled on the piazza just before breakfast.

When this occurred word was swiftly and silently conveyed over the household and all persons belonging to the domestic staff instantly gathered in the hall and doorway.

"Why, what on earth is the matter with them?" Miss Campbell asked uneasily. "Will you please look: the entire household collected in the front hall."

Mr. Campbell was as much at a loss as his cousin.

"They look as if they were going to play a joke on us," observed Billie, "Did you ever see anything so guileless and simple-hearted as they are?"

"Oh, I know what it is," cried Mary, clasping her hands with delight. "There," she said, pointing to the old gardener, who was approaching by way of one of the paths. There was an inimitable smile on his face, and he carried tenderly and gingerly a double handful of brown branches on which clustered delicate pink blossoms.

"It's the cherry blossoms! They are in bloom!" Mary shouted in her enthusiasm. "That's why they are all so delighted. The dears! They are just like a lot of children."

The crown of the year for the Japanese had indeed arrived, the season when every cherry tree becomes a magnificent nosegay which has caught the sunset's glow, and all the world goes forth to view the splendid sight.

The love of these people, young and old and of all classes, for flowers, and particularly for cherry blossoms, is touching in its simplicity and sincerity.

The old gardener was himself a delightful picture in his blue cotton, tunic-like coat, queer, tight-fitting trousers and an enormous hat that resembled an inverted flower basket. Against the coarse blue of his tunic rested the delicate rosy cloud of blossoms. With an elaborate bow he presented Mr. Campbell and each of the ladies with a branch. "Him muchly more big soon all same," he said.

"Thank you, Saiki. They are very beautiful," said Miss Campbell, speaking in the distinct, loud tone she used for persons not understanding her own language.

The girls exclaimed and admired and Mr. Campbell was delighted. He felt a kind of reverence for the old man's simple unaffected love of beauty. In the meantime, the regiment of servants who had witnessed and enjoyed the ceremony of presenting the first cherry blossoms to the master and mistress of the house retired to their various occupations.

The pleasure and surprise of the foreigners over the beauty of the cherry blossoms would be a memory for these humble people to cherish all their lives. Perhaps they had never seen the like before, these honorable barbarians; certainly nothing so perfect as the double blossom, of a delicacy and shade not to be surpassed.

Later at the breakfast table Billie concocted a scheme.

"Papa," she began, "can't we take the 'Comet' and go sight-seeing? It would be such fun, and while the 'rikshas are very nice, we are so separated, we can't all sympathize together as we usually do."

"A kind of sympathy in detachments, is it?" asked Mr. Campbell. "But I wanted to go with you on your first ride in the 'Comet.' I don't know just how the people will take to a girl's driving a red 'devil-wagon,' as they call it."

"Why not let Komatsu go along?"

"What do you think, Cousin?" asked Mr. Campbell.

Up to this time Miss Campbell had kept out of the discussion. The truth is, she yearned to relieve the tedium of life by taking a trip in the red motor car.

"Couldn't you get away and go with us?"

"Impossible this afternoon, because I have an appointment to meet some very distinguished persons to discuss various plans. One can hardly be polite enough as it is in this good-mannered country, and it would never do to break an engagement. In another week or so I shall be free to take the ladies on excursions."

"What is it all about, Papa?" asked Billie.

"Oh, government improvements, child. Things that are too important to be talked about." He pinched her cheek. "Well, beautiful American ladies, if you take Komatsu with you as interpreter and protector, guide and friend, I think you might be trusted to make a little cherry-blossom excursion in the 'Comet.' Only don't go too far or too fast and on your life don't run over anything, even a chicken, or there'll be trouble for all concerned."

So it was settled, and after breakfast Billie rushed to the mysterious back premises of the place on the other side of the house, where various hitherto unsuspected industries seemed to be in progress. There was a kitchen garden hidden by a hedge of althea bushes, a chicken yard, and in a most picturesque building, used by the Spears for a carriage house, the "Comet." So far they had been unable to find a chauffeur, and Mr. Campbell himself had gone over all the machinery and put it in order. Billie cranked up, and, jumping into her old accustomed place, guided the motor car into the open. Komatsu came at a run from around the side of the house. He was so amazed at sight of Billie in the chauffeur's seat that he could not conceal his feelings.

"Komatsu, we want you to go with us to-day. We want you to show us the cherry trees in Tokyo and Uyeno Park. I suppose we couldn't get to all the famous cherry blossom places in one afternoon?"

"Him fast runner. No sakura all same see."

"No, no. We shall go quite slowly. We want to see everything."

In less than an hour the *hanami*, signifying in Japanese a picnic to a famous place to view certain flowers in season, conducted on the most modern lines in a red motor car, proceeded on its way. Komatsu, a strangely incongruous figure, sat on the front seat beside Billie.

On the way to Tokyo the "Comet" created a sensation. All the varied wayfarers on that picturesque highway paused and stared, pointing and gesticulating.

The city was a vision of beauty. Most of its broad avenues are lined with close set rows of cherry trees which were now bursting into blossom in all the most delicate and exquisite shades of pink known to nature. Komatsu guided them about the city with a kind of pleased and gratified delight as if he were showing his own property. Sometimes he stood up and pointed to the feathery tops of carefully nurtured cherry trees, glimpses of which could be seen over the high walls surrounding private gardens.

The motorists were fairly bewildered by the beauty of it all. It was like a vast conservatory with the roof taken off. Nothing could have been more exotic or more lovely than the vista through the park with the white peak of Fujiyama, queen of mountains, glistening in the distance.

Moreover, this little jaunt in the car had stirred their blood into action. They felt once more the call of the road, the fever to be going. The old accustomed sensation that they must make a certain place by such and such a time had returned. They were of one opinion, this party of Motor-Gypsies: to go back home until sunset would be a foolish waste of golden hours. Their five wishes accorded like the notes of an harmonious chord and presently Billie, influenced by the force of this silent opinion, exclaimed:

"Suppose we take a country road and eat lunch later at some wayside tea house?"

"Splendid!" cried the others almost before she had finished.

Miss Campbell raised one feeble objection - something about the weather - but it was promptly overridden by her relative at the wheel, and presently she settled down in her seat and abandoned herself to the joy of motion.

"In all the ten thousands of miles we have covered in this car," she remarked, "I never was happier than I am at this moment."

"Why can't we go to the Arakawa Ridge?" suggested Mary, consulting a guide book. "It's only seven miles from here on the Sumida River and there are miles and miles of road bordered by double-flowering cherry trees."

This was agreeable to all concerned, and, accordingly, Komatsu guided them to this famous spot, the pride of Tokyo. On the way they passed hundreds of people in jinrikshas or on foot. Many of the pedestrians carried paper parasols and fans, exactly like the chorus in the "Mikado." Those who rode in the graceful little two-wheeled buggies looked out upon the world with expressions of calm enjoyment.

The "Comet" was a conspicuous object as it progressed slowly along the road, but so far all things worked together for good and there was no cause for uneasiness. At a little roadside tea house they paused for lunch. The building was nothing more than a shed with a low-hanging thatched roof and sides made of coarse strips of matting joined together with bamboo sticks. Humble as it was it possessed a peculiar charm, all its own. They were presently to find that the rear of the tea house facing a little garden was glorified into something rich and strange by a magnificent azalea bush in full bloom. It reached to the roof of the house and was a mass of deep red blossoms.

The ear was left in a pine grove near the house, and following Komatsu along a rocky path they presently found themselves in this delectable little garden. Here they were met by an old man and his wife, a very aged couple whose gentle deprecating expressions almost moved Miss Campbell to tears.

"The adorable old things," she exclaimed. "They remind me of two old turtle doves."

Close at their heels came two little maids who conducted the ladies into the tea house and brought tea for temporary refreshment, while Komatsu consulted with the proprietor regarding lunch.

Presently one of the little maids hurried in and placed a menu in front of Miss Campbell.

"Me speak little honorable American language," she said. "You like all same American food? Will gracious lady make eyes to look?"

Miss Campbell raised her lorgnette and examined the menu while the small maid backed away and disappeared, in the throes of extreme shyness over her endeavors.

"Girls," said Miss Campbell, in a curious, strained voice, "don't any of you dare to laugh because of course they are all peeping at us from somewhere, but I want you all to make eyes to look at this amazing production."

They crowded about her and over her shoulder read the following menu:

> *Soup by egge*
> *Eels to rice*
> *Seaweed*
> *Podadoe Sweete*
> *Sponge boiled*
> *Doormats a la U. S.*

There were tears of laughter in Miss Campbell's eyes and her voice was so shaky she could hardly trust herself to speak, even when she saw the little maid returning around the corner of the azalea bush. The faces of the four girls were crimson with suppressed laughter.

"Very nice, my dear," said Miss Campbell, "you may bring in luncheon as soon as you can."

After she had gone there was a brief but eloquent silence.

"Do, some one, make a joke," whispered Elinor.

At that moment a strange looking bob-tailed cat walked by.

"There," cried Nancy, and they all instantly burst into hysterical laughter.

"In the name of good health and excellent digestion, tell me what are doormats?" asked Billie.

"Dear knows," answered her cousin, "but I think if they must be eaten it would be best to take boiled sponges afterward."

The luncheon was purely Japanese, in spite of the English menu, and it was really excellent.

"I never thought to come to eels," Miss Campbell observed, but she enjoyed her portion, nevertheless.

"Doormats a la U. S." turned out to be a sweet cake with a sugary icing.

"I believe they were intended for doughnuts," observed that astute little person, Mary Price, and no doubt she was quite right.

When the feast was over Miss Campbell paid the bill, which was pathetically small, since there was no charge for tea and sweetmeats.

"How do we give the tip?" she asked.

"I know," answered Billie, "Papa taught me about that the other day." She consulted her note book. Tearing out a leaf, she wrapped up what would amount to about a dollar in American money, then with her little silver pencil she wrote on the package "On chadai." "That means 'honorable money for tea,'" she explained.

Next she clapped her hands. All through the house voices could be heard calling "Hai! Hai!"

Presently the maid appeared hanging her head humbly. Billie motioned to her that she wished the proprietor, who, indeed, was close at hand. With an expression of much surprise he received the chadai and bowing to the ground murmured something which Komatsu explained meant honorable thanks for poor insignificant service.

Each guest on departing received a fan as a souvenir; because, as they were to learn before they left Japan, no Japanese ever receives a present without giving another in return. Every person attached to the tea house went out to see the departure of the car, and the old woman clutched her husband's arm fearfully when she heard the vibrations of the machinery and saw Billie turn the "Comet" down the hillside to the main road.

At last, fortified by strange if not unpalatable food and thoroughly enjoying themselves, they arrived at the entrance to the magnificent avenue called Arakawa Ridge, along each side of which, as far as the eye could see, ran two rows of cherry trees in full bloom.

The avenue was lined with 'rikshas, and hundreds of pedestrians paced slowly along. They were in holiday attire and the bright colors of the kimonos and obis made a bewildering and brilliant picture. At intervals booths had been erected, decorated with lanterns, where refreshments were sold, and nearby a roving band of musicians and dancers were entertaining the crowd.

The mistake Billie made was to attempt to take the car through the crowded road where apparently there were only pedestrians and jinrikshas. But Komatsu had not objected and since they had been accustomed to take the "Comet" wherever there was a navigable road, they pushed innocently on. As for the populace celebrating the cherry blossom festival, they evidently regarded the sight of a young woman driving a red devil-wagon as something just short of miraculous. Slowly and at a dignified pace the motor car moved along the avenue, and suddenly like a bolt from the blue two things happened.

A little boy escaped from his sister's hand and ran across the road. Billie reversed the lever just as the child fell under the wheels. At the same instant a tire on a rear wheel exploded with a loud report.

Miss Campbell groaned and hid her face in her hands.

Instantly they were surrounded by a mob of angry people.

CHAPTER VII.

A BAD QUARTER OF AN HOUR.

In the uncertainty of that terrible moment everything turned black before Billie's eyes.

"I am a murderer," was all she could think. "I've killed a little child."

When the mists had cleared away she saw a weird scene about her: hundreds of Japanese men and women, speaking in low angry voices which somehow reminded her of the breaking of the surf on the beach - perhaps because the Japanese language has a sing-song rhythm. The little boy, apparently limp and lifeless, lay in his sister's arms. Komatsu had leapt clear over the front of the car and pushed his way through the people gathered about them. With a hand as skillful as a doctor's he felt the child's pulse and placed his ear over his heart.

"Baby only make believe dead," he said. "Honorable heart beating all same like steam engine."

At these hopeful words Miss Campbell came to herself with a start. For a moment she had been faint and sick with the notion of what had happened. Never before in all their thousands of miles of touring in the "Comet" had they injured so much as a fly; and now to run down a little child! It was too dreadful to contemplate.

"Komatsu," she ordered, in an unsteady voice, "tell the girl to get in and we will take her brother to the nearest doctor."

Komatsu conveyed this message to the stricken sister, who shook her head violently.

"Honorable devil-wagon shoot pistol. Japanese no likee," he said.

Closer and closer pressed the tense mob about the party. These courteous and gentle Japanese had suddenly been transformed into a fierce, savage people.

From one end of Japan to the other a child is considered a sacred thing. If Billie had injured a grown person the public sentiment would not have been so strong, but to harm one of these little "treasure flowers" was to strike at the very heart of the nation.

"Can't you understand that we are sorry and anxious to help you?" cried Miss Campbell, addressing the mob, but her voice was lost in the subdued threatening murmur which sounded like distant thunder heralding the approach of a storm.

"Good heavens, Komatsu, what are we to do? The child might be saved if they would only listen to reason."

"People no likee honorable devil-wagon. Going breaking little pieces all same like sticks."

"No, no, they must not," ejaculated Billie. "We are sorry," she cried, stretching out her hands appealingly to the circle of Japanese pressed around the car. "We didn't mean to do it."

In the meantime Miss Campbell had produced her bottle of smelling salts, the same that had accompanied her on all her trips, and climbed out of the car. With a motion imperious and compelling she pushed aside the men and women in the circle.

The sister had laid the child on the ground and was kneeling beside him.

Komatsu knelt on the other side, feeling the little legs and body.

"No break bones," he said briefly.

Miss Campbell sat on the ground by the unconscious child, wondering vaguely if she would ever rise again.

"They may tear us to pieces before we get back. They are like an angry, silent pack of wolves," she thought to herself. "Komatsu," she said aloud, "I believe he has fainted from fright," She put the smelling bottle to the baby's funny snub nose.

Presently the boy opened his eyes.

At this moment from the midst of the crowd there came a strange shrill cry and a distracted looking woman began beating and fighting her way toward the group.

"Honorable mother come in big hurry," said Komatsu, in a low voice. "Gracious lady, take jinriksha. Honorable quickness best now."

"But the child isn't injured, Komatsu. Look, he's opened his eyes and he's going to sit up. It was simply fright."

"No like honorable devil-wagon," went on Komatsu steadily.

While this low, rapid dialogue was taking place Billie, standing on the front seat of the "Comet" on the lookout for help, saw something that made her blood turn cold. A band of fierce looking young men in Japanese costume was approaching on the run. The leader was brandishing a short knife with a two-edged glittering blade and the others flourished sword canes. Billie was thankful that Miss Campbell was too much occupied at that moment in assuring the poor mother that her child was not injured to notice this murderous looking company. Komatsu had quietly placed himself beside the car, faithful soul, ready to die in the service of his ladies.

Were they all going to be cut to pieces or was only the "Comet" to be sacrificed in revenge for the accident?

The Motor Maids exchanged frightened glances.

"If I only knew six words in Japanese," thought Billie.

"Make honorable quickness to descend, gracious lady. Come, come," Komatsu urged. "To jinriksha. Leave red devil-wagon. This place no good for staying in."

"Oh, Komatsu, try and reason with them," pleaded Billie. "We don't want to lose the 'Comet,' It wasn't his fault. He was going quite slowly. He didn't mean to hurt the little boy. He's the kindest hearted old thing. It wasn't anybody's fault. Can't you tell them that?"

Billie was too distracted and unhappy to realize how absurd her words might have sounded to any English-speaking person. It had always seemed to her that a real heart beat somewhere in the mechanical organism of the red motor. Gasoline was his life's blood and his pulse-beats were only the throb of the engine, but, to Billie, he was a faithful and devoted soul and she was not quite prepared to say what she would do in order to save him from destruction.

However, at the moment that the band of young men, scarcely more than boys any of them, reached the car, some one sprang into the machine from the other side.

Turning quickly, Billie was confronted by a tall, slender young woman in a white serge suit and a big black hat. She had a dark, creamy complexion, dark eyes that slanted slightly and hair of a queer mousy shade of brown.

"Wait," said the stranger, "I will speak to them," and mounting the seat, she addressed the crowd in their own tongue with extraordinary fluency, the girls thought, remembering what they had heard concerning the difficulties of that language. There was an elegance and fascination indescribable about the stranger. Nancy recognized her instantly as the lady in the garden. Miss Campbell knew her as Mme. Fontaine, newspaper correspondent. The others in the party imagined her to be almost anything romantic and interesting; perhaps a foreign princess; a great actress; something remarkable, surely.

In a beautiful, cultured voice, far reaching in spite of its soft tones, she harangued the multitude which little by little fell back. The group of fierce young men put away their weapons and disappeared in the mob. The little boy, the cause of all the trouble, was now standing on his feet blinking his eyes at Miss Campbell. How the picture was stamped on their minds like a vividly colored print!

Miss Campbell took out her purse and gave the mother of the boy some money. Being still quite ignorant of Japanese coinage she did not pause to make any laborious calculations, but poured all the money in the purse into the woman's outstretched hand. It must have been an undreamed-of sum, for the mother's face was wreathed in delighted smiles. She bowed until her forehead almost touched the ground, as did the witnesses of this princely generosity.

"It's all over now," said Mme. Fontaine, stepping down from the seat and smiling at Billie. "You had a bad quarter of an hour, though, I fear."

"I don't know how we can ever thank you," exclaimed Billie. "You not only saved the car from destruction, but you may have saved us, too. There's no telling how far they would have gone once they got started."

"No, no, they would not have harmed you, but they might have injured the car. They are a good deal like children, but they are not butchers. I think they admired your courage, too, for not deserting the sinking ship."

Miss Campbell now approached and held out her hand gratefully.

"You are heaping coals of fire on my head, Mme. Fontaine," she said. "Yesterday I refused to grant you a favor and to-day you are placing us everlastingly in your debt."

"No, no, you must not put it that way," said the other woman, with a graceful movement of protest. "You were quite right not to be interviewed if you did not wish it. Some Americans do not object to publicity, you know. One can never tell. But what I did just now any other person who spoke both languages would have been glad to do."

The end of the episode was that Mme. Fontaine waited with Miss Campbell and the three girls, while Billie, in the center of a curious circle of onlookers and with the help of Komatsu, put on a new tire.

"Are you in a 'riksha?" asked Miss Campbell of their deliverer. "We would be glad if you would let us take you back to Tokyo in the car. My young cousin is a careful and experienced chauffeur. This is the only accident of the sort we have ever had and I think it was entirely the fault of the child."

"Oh, I am not in the least timid in motor cars and I accept with pleasure," answered Mme. Fontaine quickly.

Some twenty minutes later, with Komatsu running ahead to clear the road, the "Comet" threaded his way at a snail's pace along the Arakawa Ridge. No doubt his mechanical organism, which Billie had endowed with a soul, heaved a sigh of relief when they took the road home.

"Who were the young men with the knives and sword canes, Mme. Fontaine?" asked Mary on the way back.

"Oh, they are a group of fanatical young persons opposed to foreigners.

Most of them are descendants of the samurai. They believe in old Japan. They talk the wildest kind of nonsense, and while their beliefs are opposed to progress, they represent in Japan what the Nihilists represent in Russia and the Anarchists and such people in other countries. They will outgrow it in time. Some of the finest men in Japan once belonged to these clubs of *soshi*, as they are called. In another generation there will be very few of them left. In the meantime they are quite dangerous occasionally. About fifty years ago a band of them attacked the English Legation at Takanawa and there was a fierce fight. But I feel perfectly sure that they wouldn't attack people now. Only motor cars and the like."

"That would have been bad enough," remarked Billie, patting the wheel of the "Comet."

Mme. Fontaine smiled pleasantly.

"After the great excitement may I not have the pleasure of offering you a reviving cup of tea at my house? It would make me very happy."

Miss Campbell would have much preferred to go straight home, but to decline the invitation would have seemed ungracious and she accepted promptly.

Along the broad streets of Tokyo, under out-stretched boughs heavy with blossoms, they rolled, and at last Billie paused as directed at a gate in a wall behind which was a charming little house, set in the usual beautiful garden.

If Mme. Fontaine was fascinating and elegant, so also was her home. The drawing-room, which seemed to occupy most of the second floor, was furnished in European fashion with deep chairs and couches, Oriental rugs and rich hangings. There was a grand piano near the windows, and on the walls were the rarest and most beautiful Japanese prints. It was a blending of the East and West and was one of the most artistic and delightful apartments the girls had ever seen. In the dim shadowy confines they caught glimpses of teakwood cabinets in which were carved ivories and pieces of fine porcelain. The girls would have liked well to linger another hour among all these interesting and strange objects, but Miss Campbell, for some reason, was in her most conventional mood. While her manner toward Mme. Fontaine left nothing to be desired and she was graciousness personified, she cut the call to twenty-five minutes by the French clock on the mantel, and then go she would. As they were leaving Mary noticed on a table near the door two splendid swords, one very large and heavy and one with a double-edged blade of much smaller size.

"Oh, are these the swords of a samurai warrior?" she demanded, with excited interest.

"Yes," answered Mme. Fontaine. "They belonged to my great grandfather."

Not until they were back in the "Comet" and well on the way home did they realize the meaning of her words.

"Then," exclaimed Nancy, "she is half Japanese."

"And I've invited her to dine the day after tomorrow," Miss Campbell remarked irrelevantly.

The adventure on Arakawa Ridge was far-reaching in its results as a matter of fact, but the most immediate one was a severe punishment administered by that usually kind and gentle person, Mr. Campbell, on no less a victim than the "Comet." Just what the punishment was you will find out when the Motor Maids themselves discover it.

CHAPTER VIII.

THE COMPASSIONATE GOD, JIZU.

Miss Campbell was very dubious about having invited Mme. Fontaine to dine.

"Of course she was very kind," she remarked, "and we owe her a great deal, but I wish we could show our appreciation in some other way. We don't know anything about her: who she is; where she came from; whether she has any family."

"But, my dear cousin," said Mr. Campbell, who had wandered about the world so much that he was accustomed to taking people without any questions, "what difference does it make? You say she is refined and well-bred. We know she is kind because of what she did for us. But I will make some inquiries about her if you like -"

"I never liked mixed bloods," interrupted Miss Campbell, not listening to her relation.

"Everybody has some mixture of bloods," laughed Billie. "Look at Mary - French and English; look at Elinor - Scotch and Irish."

"No, no," protested Miss Campbell "Those aren't the kinds of mixtures I referred to. It's those queer Oriental bloods - yellow people and white people."

The others all smiled indulgently. Miss Campbell was just a little old-fashioned lady with old-fashioned restricted views, they thought. She was the only one of the motor party who had not fallen under the spell of Mme. Fontaine, and apparently the only cause for her objection was because this charming stranger was part Japanese and wrote for the newspapers.

That evening Mr. Campbell endeavored to set her fears at rest.

"I have inquired about your mysterious Mme. Fontaine," he said. "She is a widow. Her husband was editor of a paper in Shanghai. She herself is a writer and a newspaper correspondent. She has written several novels published in Shanghai, and she is generally considered to be a very bright person. She has been living in Tokyo not quite a year and goes out very little."

This fragment of her history only seemed to deepen the atmosphere of romance which enveloped the "Widow of Shanghai," as Mr. Campbell would call her, and the Motor Maids rather eagerly awaited the evening when she was to dine with them.

In the meantime, they were to receive a ceremonious call from the family of Yoritomo Ito, and he himself was to act as interpreter for the three Japanese ladies, his mother, his aunt and his sister. They appeared one afternoon in two jinrikshas and such a bowing and smiling was never seen before. The day had been sultry and hot and tea was served in the summer-house in the garden by the little maids attached to the household. Miss Campbell was sorry that the pretty Onoye, flower of the staff, did not appear. However, these things were all left to O'Haru, and she said nothing.

Yoritomo's sister, O'Kami San (that is to say: the honorable Miss Kami), spoke a very little English. This fact she had bashfully hidden from the girls on the occasion of their first meeting. But when Billie, through Yoritomo, asked his sister to walk in the garden, she answered herself:

"Receive thanks. Honorable walk will confer pleasure."

Assuredly the Japanese-English dictionaries and phrase books must all use the most stilted and ceremonious English words, so Billie thought.

"'Receive thanks and confer pleasure!' How absurd!"

But then Billie did not realize that the Japanese language abounds in such ceremonious words and high-sounding phrases and, in order to keep the spirit of the original, translations are generally literal.

Off they trooped down a garden path, followed by the reproachful eyes of Miss Helen Campbell, who found it a decided strain on the nerves to keep a second-hand conversation going. Nancy lingered behind and helped her out by giving Yoritomo an account of their accident on Arakawa Ridge. This he immediately passed on to his mother and aunt.

In the meantime, O'Kami San, trotting along beside Billie, with Mary and Elinor following behind, might have just stepped out of a Japanese fan. She was so entirely unreal and cunning that the girls had no eyes for the rosy rain of cherry blossoms dropping from the trees, nor the lovely vista of garden with its flaming bushes of azaleas and cool green clumps of ferns. Out of compliment to the season O'Kami San wore a robe of delicate pink embroidered all over with sprays of cherry blossoms in deeper shades. Her obi, or sash, was of pale green silk. Her hair was elaborately pompadoured and drawn up in the back into a large glossy roll held in place with tortoise shell pins. No doubt it had taken hours to arrange; two, at the very least.

Billie patted her own smooth rolls serenely.

"Suppose I had to sleep with my neck on a little wooden bench every night to preserve my *coiffure*," she thought. "I think I'd just lay my head on the executioner's block and say, 'Strike it off. It's not worth the trouble.'"

"Think garden pretty, O'Kami San?" began Mary, whose method of talking with the Japanese was to preserve only the framework of a sentence and drop all articles and small words.

"Much pretty. Me - like honorable garden and beautiful American ladee," answered O'Kami, speaking slowly and distinctly.

English pronunciation never seemed to trouble the Japanese. It was only choice of words and construction.

"What do you do all day, O'Kami San?" asked Elinor.

"Much honorable work," answered the Japanese girl. "Cooking; sew-ing"; she pointed to her kimono; "mu-seek; book-stu-dee. Ah, much work to become wife."

"You are not thinking of marrying, surely? Your brother says you are only sixteen," protested Mary.

O'Kami nodded her head and smiled.

"Arrange all the day before to this."

"Do you love him?" asked Mary, in an awed tone of voice.

O'Kami looked puzzled. The word "love" she had not learned.

"O'Kami much happy. Honorable mother of husband not any more. Gone." She pointed up.

"Goodness!" broke in Elinor. "She means that there will be no mother-in-law, so the marriage is sure to be a happy one. What a mother-in-law ridden place this country is!"

She spoke too rapidly for the Japanese girl to grasp the meaning of any word except "mother-in-law."

"Mother-in-law," she repeated slowly. "Little Japanese girl

much afraid to great mother-in-law."

The girls laughed and O'Kami's silvery note mingled with theirs.

"I found something quite new and interesting in the garden the other day," observed Mary. "Or rather not quite new, but quite old. Who wants to see it?"

"Lead on, Macduff," ordered Billie.

"It's an old shrine," continued Mary. "Komatsu says it's to the Compassionate God, Jizu. He's sitting cross-legged in a little niche in the hillside below the bridge and he has a beautiful frame of clematis vines around him. I think he's delightful."

O'Kami San was unable to grasp the meaning of this rapid fire of words, at least it seemed to her to be a rapid fire. Most people are under the impression that a foreign language is spoken faster than their own. But she trotted along beside the others, always with the same polite, intelligent smile, as if she understood every word.

Having crossed the bridge, they followed a narrow path through a grove of pine trees. The path took an unexpected curve to the right and led them around the side of a grassy embankment under which sat the stone image of the Compassionate God, Jizu. The inscrutable smile of the nation hovered on the lips of the ancient idol, and his compassionate stone eyes looked out upon the green little world around him with a gentle tolerance. Time and tempests had worn away his arms and softened the outlines of his stone countenance. He was indeed a graven image of kindly mien and of a certain majesty of expression.

But there was, another visitor at the shrine of the Compassionate God. She lay flat on her face in a tumbled, many-colored little heap before the gray old image at whose feet was her offering: a pitiful little bunch of wild roses. She had been sobbing. It was easy to tell. The storm of weeping had passed now and she lay quite still, but at intervals there was that catch in the breath which follows a period of bitter crying.

The three American girls paused at the edge of the miniature lawn about the shrine and exchanged embarrassed glances. O'Kami Sail drew back a step or two. It was their intention to creep away as noiselessly as possible and leave the unhappy worshiper at the shrine none the wiser that she had been observed by profane, foreign eyes. But at this moment a temple bell not far off sent out a clear silver note in the stillness. The bright-colored heap stirred into life and the sorrowful worshiper rose and looked about her bewildered.

It was Onoye, as they had suspected, and Mary recalled that it was the second time she had seen the Japanese girl crying miserably when she thought she was alone.

Onoye tried to smile when she saw the three young ladies of the house looking at her with great concern. She ran to Billie and fell on her knees.

"Forgive, gracious lady," she said, endeavoring to compose her expression to its usual tranquility.

"Why, you poor dear, what have I to forgive?" exclaimed Billie, trying to raise Onoye to her feet.

"Why are you so unhappy, Onoye? Is there anything we can do for you?" asked Elinor.

"Do tell us and let us help you," put in Mary.

But Onoye was silent.

"O'Kami San, will you not ask her?" said Billie. "Perhaps she would tell you in Japanese when she can't in English."

At the words "O' Kami San," Onoye jumped to her feet in

subdued excitement.

"O'Kami San," she repeated.

The two Japanese girls confronted each other. They spoke in low, rapid voices and their faces were so calm and unemotional they might have been two Japanese dolls wound tip to move the lips and occasionally make a slight gesture with one hand. Presently Onoye slipped from her *obi* a small package done up in crêpe paper and gave it to O'Kami, who concealed it in the voluminous folds of her own kimono. They exchanged low, ceremonious bows and Onoye hurried away, while O'Kami turned to the mystified young-Americans with an apologetic smile.

"Receive excuses and pardon grant," she said.

Billie made a superhuman effort not to laugh, while Mary stooped to break off a spray of azaleas and Elinor examined intently a stunted pine tree planted in a big green jar near the path.

Japanese gardeners are very fond of cultivating these dwarf trees. Some of the tiniest are said to be of great age. The arrested development contorts the venerable branches into strange twisted forms but they put forth blossoms and foliage with systematic dignity.

"What is the matter with our little maid? Were you able to find out?" Billie asked the visitor.

But O'Kami San was not inclined to be communicative, and they were obliged to return to the summer-house with their curiosity entirely unsatisfied. In the meantime, Miss Campbell and Nancy were in a painful state of embarrassment about what to say next. The conversation had come to a dead stop, while Miss Campbell, with a flushed face, raised her eyes to heaven with a prayerful look and Nancy endeavored to say a few words about the weather. Yoritomo was inclined to be silent, too. He kept his eyes on the floor and only raised them to transmit Miss Campbell's remarks to his mother and aunt.

"Will you ask your mother, Mr. Ito, if - she suffers from rheumatism from sitting on the floor so much?" asked Miss Campbell, groaning mentally and sending up a prayer that the visitors would see fit to bring the visit to an immediate end.

There was a short colloquy between mother and son, during which Mme. Ito smiled blandly and waved her fan to and fro.

"No, Madam, my mother does not have that complaint," answered her son in precise English.

Miss Campbell flashed a glance of black reproach at Nancy, as much as to say:

"It's your turn now, ungrateful girl. Speak, for heaven's sake."

Nancy exchanged a hopeless glance with the distracted lady. Then she remarked:

"Mr. Ito, is your aunt married?"

Yoritomo smiled broadly.

"She is a widow," he replied. "In Japan all widows cut their hair short."

"But what a strange custom," objected Nancy. "That would keep them from ever marrying a second time. I'm sure I should never cut my hair if my husband died. I should use hair tonic to make it grow longer and thicker."

Yoritomo laughed outright and communicated Nancy's views to his relatives. They laughed, too, and contemplated her knot of chestnut curls with much admiration.

There came another uncomfortable pause. Two simultaneous

winged prayers went up into the ether and relief was granted in an unexpected and startling guise. Billie and her friends had just returned and tea and refreshments of a light volatile nature were being passed for the fourth time, by order of Miss Campbell. The visitors were elaborately declining all further nourishment when Nancy saw an arm raised from behind a thick clump of shrubbery near the summer-house. It was clothed in nondescript brown and long fingers clutched a stone. The arm gave a swift circular movement, as if to gain impetus. Then it went backward with a movement of a pitcher about to throw a ball.

"Yoritomo," shrieked Nancy, for the stone seemed to be aimed straight at his head.

In the fraction of an instant the young Japanese had ducked and the stone had crashed into the summer-house and fallen at his feet, making a dent in the floor.

Undoubtedly Nancy had saved his life.

"Oh, oh, oh!" cried Miss Campbell, but Mme. Ito and her sister and daughter were perfectly calm and silent, as were also the Japanese maids, gathered in a frightened group behind them.

"I never saw people take on so little," Miss Campbell observed later, describing the incident to her cousin.

Nancy wept softly. It was never very difficult for her to weep and she emerged from one of these gentle paroxysms - even as the flowers after a summer rain - a little dewy but refreshed.

Yoritomo vaulted over the rail of the summer-house and ran in the direction of the group of shrubbery. But, of course, no one was there. Who could expect an assassin to wait and be caught?

"I think we had better get into the house at once," ordered Miss Campbell, and taking Mme. Ito's arm, she hurried the little lady up the path, calling to the others to follow. Once in the drawing-room, all the windows were ordered closed and the doors locked, while Komatsu was sent to search the premises.

"What is your opinion, Mr. Ito?" asked Billie. "Was it an enemy of yours or some one who wanted to exterminate us because we are foreigners?"

But Yoritomo could not enlighten her.

"I cannot say," was all they could get out of him.

He was only deeply chagrined, as was his mother, that the American ladies should have been subjected to such treatment in Japan.

The Campbell party finally arrived at the conclusion that it was an insane person, and Mr. Campbell immediately engaged a day and night watchman and reported the matter to the police.

CHAPTER IX.

A BIRTHDAY PARTY.

It so happened that the dinner to Mme. Fontaine became a triple celebration. Billie recalled that it was her father's birthday, for one thing.

"He's forgotten it himself," she said. "He never did remember that he was entitled to a birthday."

Furthermore, it was the occasion always of great rejoicing in Japan, being the fifth day of the fifth month on which the Boys' Festival - *O Sekku*, as it is called there - is celebrated.

"Think of my sweet old boy being born on this lucky day!" cried Billie.- "Why can't we give him a real Japanese surprise party, Cousin Helen, and invite those nice men to come? Mr. Ito will tell us what to do."

When Mr. Campbell departed for Tokyo that lovely morning on the fifth of May he had no idea of the plans that were hatching in his home. Scarcely had his 'riksha disappeared down the road, when the entire household became actively busy. Komatsu made a hurried visit to town, bearing notes of invitation to the few acquaintances of the Campbells and returned later in the day accompanied by two men carrying large bales on their backs. That evening when the master of the house returned in time to dress for dinner he scarcely recognized his abode, which had been decorated in a most extraordinary manner.

Across the front of the house on long poles were at least six enormous paper carp, which rose and fell and became realistically inflated with every passing breeze. Very fantastic they appeared with their gaping mouths, their enormous bulging eyes and fins and their scales shining in the sunlight.

The carp, it must be known, is the sacred emblem of the male child in Japan. It also signifies courage, endurance and other admirable though not exclusively masculine qualities. This valiant fish can accomplish the difficult feat of swimming up the rapids, even as a brave youth must conquer difficulties and surmount obstacles. His name is synonymous with perseverance and fortitude. The fifth of May is every boy's birthday in Japan, no matter what his real birthday is, and on that day a feast is kept in every home, rich or poor, where there is a son.

"I suppose, because we have only one son in our house, we are entitled to only one carp," observed Billie, "but I think our nice old boy is good enough for us to string up twenty carp."

This statement was unanimously acceded to by all persons connected with the feast.

All the afternoon the girls had worked over the decorations. The garden was strung with lanterns much more beautiful and artistic in design than any that ever reach America; and the house, under the supervision of Onoye and her mother, was made beautiful with the splendid iris in all its varying shades from deep purple to pale mauve. Among their long, slender, delicate leaves the flowers seemed to be growing in the shallow dishes in which devices of soft lead held them in place.

"Are we entertaining a family of sons this evening or have we just decided to celebrate whether we have sons or not?" asked Mr. Campbell, greeting his daughter on the piazza.

"We are entertaining for our only son, the most promising and delightful young man in the entire universe," answered Billie, kissing him.

"I always thought you were a singularly fortunate young man, Duncan," remarked Miss Campbell, "but I shall no longer attribute it entirely to industry, intelligence and good looks."

"What's the reason, then, Cousin Helen?" asked Mr. Campbell, laughing.

"Why, have you forgotten, boy, that this is your birthday? Forty-five years old, and you don't remember it!"

"I did forget it," said Mr. Campbell, "but I don't see where the luck comes in."

They explained the meaning of the Boys' Festival and the lucky coincidence that had brought him into the world on that auspicious day.

"Go in now and get dressed, for the Widow of Shanghai will be arriving pretty soon and other company besides," ordered Billie.

The girls had dressed early and their pretty summer frocks gleamed softly against the green of the shrubbery as they flitted about the garden and the lawn in the twilight. Nancy was wearing her first train that night; it was only a wee bit of a train, nothing regal and sweeping; but it gave her a secret thrill to throw it over one arm, displaying her lace trimmed petticoat underneath, while she tripped along the garden path. The dress was of pink batiste and delicate lace, and from the round neck her throat rose soft and white like a column. She was the first of the four friends to wear a train. Even Elinor, tall and slender in her white lingerie frock, had not aspired to that dignity. Billie was wearing her best blue mulle that became her mightily because it was near the shade of her blue-gray eyes, and little Mary was dressed in one of the dainty muslin frocks that her mother excelled in making.

"They are no longer little girls," thought Miss Campbell, rather sadly, it must be confessed. She was sitting in a long-chair on the piazza watching her four charges flit about the lawn. "They are almost young ladies now, and how pretty they are, too; each is so different from the other and each charming in her own way. Billie, I think, is too much of a tomboy to worry about yet. Elinor is far too dignified; Mary is too shy. But I feel I shall have to keep a sharp eye on Nancy. Those blue eyes of hers are simply wells of coquetry. I believe the child would flirt with a stone. I doubt if half the time she realizes herself how eloquent she can make them. Little mischief!"

The little lady smiled indulgently, recalling her own blue eyes and the mischief they had been known to stir up.

"And now this Widow from Shanghai comes and breaks in on us," her thoughts proceeded irrelevantly. "I don't in the least wish to cultivate her friendship, but I know her kind. Once she gets her foot in the door there'll be no shaking her off."

As a matter of fact, Miss Helen Campbell, spinster, was never very enthusiastic about widows.

"I don't care for them," she used to say. "They are a knowing, designing lot."

Once when she was asked by a missionary society in West Haven to contribute to a fund for the widows in India, to induce them not to mount their husbands' funeral pyres and permit themselves to be consumed by mortuary flames, Miss Campbell indignantly refused.

"I am sure, if they are so foolish, that's much the best place for them," she announced. "I prefer to give my money for more worthy causes."

And now a widow, who, far from having mounted any funeral pyre, appeared to enjoy life immensely, had placed them under obligations.

"She is a slant-eyed widow with a yellow skin," Miss Campbell thought uncharitably, "and her hair that ought to be dark is light. Of course that isn't her fault and neither is her peculiar complexion nor her slant eyes, but I do wish she were one thing or the other and not half and half."

Of course all these inhospitable and unfriendly notions the little lady was careful to keep to herself. When presently the Widow of Shanghai rode up in a 'riksha and was helped to alight by three maids at once, Miss Campbell was all graciousness and affability.

Mme. Fontaine wore a beautiful white embroidered crêpe dinner dress. Her figure was so slender Miss Campbell feared it might sway and bend with the least breath of wind. Her curious fluffy hair was arranged on top of her head and her only ornament was a string of small pearls wound twice around her throat. They were very beautiful pearls, each one perfect to the casual eye.

"But then, who can tell the real from the unreal nowadays," thought Miss Campbell, regarding the jewels critically. "They might be imitation, every one of them."

"Reggie" Carlton, as he came to be known to the girls, and Nicholas Grimm soon followed the widow, and after them came Mr. Buxton. Yoritomo could not appear that evening, because of the celebration in his own home where he must remain and share in the family feast.

Mme. Fontaine was reserved almost to the point of shyness with the four men of the party, whom she now met for the first time. But she drew the girls around her by a kind of irresistible attraction. Billie found herself talking as freely as she talked with her three friends. The widow had a curiously sympathetic way of listening that provoked confidences. There was a good deal of friendly rivalry among the Motor Maids for her society. They took turns sitting by her side during the half hour before dinner was announced; but Nancy felt a certain superiority over the others. Was she not bound by a secret tie to this fascinating person because of their chance meeting in the garden in the rain?

"These four girls of mine seem to have acquired a monopoly over you, Mme. Fontaine," observed Mr. Campbell, just returned from a short conference with Mr. Buxton in the library. "They don't give the rest of us half a chance. They have fenced you around as if you were a sacred image of Buddha."

"I feel that they have paid me a great compliment," answered the widow, smiling, "To a lonely woman the friendship of four charming young girls is very sweet."

Mr. Campbell somehow felt extremely sorry for this lonely lady. Mr. Buxton also was touched with commiseration, and the younger men, too, were moved to cast glances of sympathy in her direction.

For the first time in her life Miss Campbell experienced the same sensation a young girl feels when she is left sitting against the wall at a dance while her friends are being whirled about. At first she thought the sensation was a touch of indigestion which frequently brings with it, its near relative, depression. But when the circle closed in around the Widow of Shanghai, and Helen Campbell, spinster, of America, was left sitting quite alone to contemplate the view, she decided that it was not indigestion nor any of its ramifications that ailed her. What the sensation was she could not name, but she felt a profound and entirely human irritation with the Widow of Shanghai and her ingratiating methods.

Fortunately dinner was announced and on the arm of Mr. Buxton she led the way to the dining room with the air of an exiled queen.

Billie was very anxious about the success of her father's birthday dinner. She had herself assisted in decorating the table, and had insisted on placing a crystal bowl of goldfish in the center, although O'Haru had told her that goldfish were not carp, and therefore had no significance whatever with the day.

However, Onoye had caught the idea at once and had carried it out charmingly. Hiding behind the screen, where she could see without being seen, her heart warmed with joy when she heard the exclamations of the guests. The center of the table was arranged to resemble a little lake. The shallow bowl of goldfish was placed on a flat round mirror, on the edge of which nodded groups of iris and their sword-like leaves planted in shallow green dishes; pebbles and water grasses hid the perforations which held them in place. Two little boats sailed on the lake, and at one side was a miniature grotto formed of rocks and moss, and spanned by a little bridge.

"Isn't it cunning?" asked Billie proudly, "and isn't Onoye clever to have carried out the scheme so perfectly?"

"She is, indeed," assented Miss Campbell, feeling suddenly glad to praise some one to counteract the unusual sensations that had possessed her a moment before.

"It is a part of every Japanese girl's education to learn the art of arranging flowers," said Mme. Fontaine. "She is taught that, just as girls in other countries are taught music and languages. It often takes several hours to arrange a group of flowers. The object is, you see, to make them look as natural as possible in the vase."

"It is a pretty accomplishment," said Miss Campbell, "but I doubt if any American girl would have the patience to learn it. Can you imagine, Billie, spending two hours arranging three lilies in a bowl to make them look as if they had grown there?"

"No, I can't," laughed Billie, "but I have spent two hours many times on my back under the 'Comet' trying to find a loose screw."

"If I had a wife -" here Nicholas remarked and paused because everybody laughed.

"Well, if you had one, what would you do with her? Beat her?" asked Mr. Buxton.

"Do I look like a wife beater?" demanded Nicholas indignantly. "No. I was going to say I'd rather she would know about loose screws in machinery than how to arrange flowers."

"You speak as if marriage was one long motor trip, my boy," observed Mr. Campbell.

"And, surely," put in Miss Campbell, "if the machinery broke down, you wouldn't compel your wife to repair it?"

"I am afraid very few girls would be eligible for your wife, Mr. Grimm," remarked Mme. Fontaine.

As for Billie, she said nothing at all, but glanced down at her plate, because Nicholas looked straight at her and then burst out with:

"Don't jump on me, everybody, with both feet. I only meant that it's a jolly fine girl who can - er - who - knows -"

He broke down in confusion.

"You mean that a young lady chauffeur would make an excellent wife?" laughed Mr. Campbell.

"Spare his blushes," put in Reggie, and then the talk shifted to other subjects.

It is customary in Japan on the day of the Boys' Festival to tell stories of the heroes of the country, and after dinner when they had gathered in the lantern-hung summer-house for coffee, Mme. Fontaine, urged by the girls, recounted an incident in the life of Yamato, or O'Osu, as he was then known. He was the son of the Emperor Keiko, and when a mere slip of a boy was sent by his father to slay two fierce robbers who had been spreading terror through the country. O'Osu gladly undertook the affair and since the outlaws were giants and he just a boy, he devised a cunning scheme to outwit the terrible brigands. He was slender and small and his hair still long, so that in the gorgeous clothes of a dancing girl no one would ever have guessed he was a brave and reckless young prince.

One night when the robbers were feasting in their cave after pillaging the country for miles around, the beautiful dancing girl appeared before them like a vision. She charmed them with her songs and dances and then suddenly she whipped out a sharp sword and slew the nearest robber. As the other fled terror-stricken to the entrance of the cave, she thrust him in the back and he fell to the ground.

"'Pause, oh Prince, for prince thou surely art,' he gasped. 'But why hast thou done this deed?'

"And the prince, standing over him with the dripping sword, said:

"'I am O'Osu, messenger of the Emperor and avenger of evil.'

"'Then,' said the dying robber, 'thou shalt have a new name. Until this hour my brother and I have been called the bravest men in the West. To thee, august boy, I bequeath the title. Let men call thee the bravest in Yamato.'

"From that day O'Osu was called 'Yamato Take,' and never did he wrong the name."

Mary sighed when Mme. Fontaine had finished the story. She yearned for the gift of language and the power to chain the attention of a circle of people. How had she done it, this mysterious foreigner who could handle the English language even better than English people? Her words were simple and gestures she used almost none. It was her voice, Mary thought.

KATHERINE STOKES

There was an undercurrent of dramatic power in it, like a subterranean river. It could only be guessed at, but it was there, powerful and deep. Even Miss Campbell, unreasonably prejudiced, felt the undercurrent.

"That is a charming story," she observed. "I suppose Japan is filled with many romantic stories of that sort."

"Hundreds of them," answered the widow. "Volumes and volumes could be written about them and still the half not be told."

"And you know many of them, I suppose?" asked Billie.

"Oh, yes. One could not live in Japan without studying her history, so filled with romances and legends of heroic deeds. It is fascinating, I assure you, and furnishes no end of subjects for decorations from a picture on a fan to the masterpiece of a great artist."

There was a moment's silence in the company of which Mme. Fontaine certainly seemed the center. She looked suddenly very Japanese. Against the white of her dress her soft skin gleamed like polished old ivory. Her eyes were darker and more noticeably slanting than ever before. If she only had had dark hair! What country had given her those strangely incongruous locks?

And now it was proposed that they should wander in the garden, and off they started by various paths and bypaths all leading eventually to the little curved bridge at the far end, where Nancy had hung two large yellow lanterns on the ends of supple willow wands.

The Widow of Shanghai walked between Billie and Mr. Campbell, but she had little to say. The moon, swinging over them like another yellow lantern, had glorified the garden into a little earthly paradise. It seemed somehow inappropriate to speak above a whisper in the midst of so much exquisite beauty. The wisteria had opened up during the day and now hung in magnificent purple clusters from an arbor across the main walk.

From the servants' quarters came the tinkle of the samisen, and a breeze laden with the scent of flowers brought with it also the distant sound of voices and laughter.

Nicholas Grimm had joined Billie, and the two young people now lingered in the arbor. In the curve of a path they caught an occasional glimpse of a white dress. The music of Nancy's laugh came to them mingled with Mary's high, sweet note. Gradually the voices died away. The garden seemed to be under a spell. Billie, sitting beside Nicholas in the arbor, waited breathlessly. Then at last in the stillness there burst forth such a stream of full-throated singing as had never been heard.

"It's a nightingale," whispered Nicholas.

Billie felt that she would like very much to cry. Nothing had ever stirred her as this flood of melody which seemed to have been turned on for their especial benefit. While they listened, there came the sound of three pistol shots in quick succession and a cry. Was it an English cry for help?

Instantly Nicholas was on his feet.

"You had better stay here," he said. "I'll run and see what has happened."

Before Billie could reply, Nancy dashed up.

"We are all to go into the house," she said. "Someone has shot a pistol in the far end of the garden. The men have gone down there."

Billie considered the situation for a moment. Certainly neither her father nor his three guests were armed. Would it not be a good precaution to go to the library and get her father's pistol? It was merely an impulse, and she could hardly explain it later, but she obeyed it.

"It's nothing serious, Mr. Buxton says. Probably someone who has been celebrating has wandered into the garden, but we had better wait for them in the house," Billie heard Miss Campbell remark, as she ran along the path to the side entrance.

CHAPTER X.

IN THE DARK.

The impulse that had moved Billie to run ahead of her friends and dash into the library for her father's pistol carried her so fast, indeed, that she was in the room with the door closed behind her before she realized what she was doing. It was perfectly dark there. Not even the brilliant moonlight outside penetrated through the heavy curtains drawn for the night.

"There are always matches on the desk," she thought, remembering that her father usually smoked while he worked over his papers.

With her hand still on the doorknob she turned and faced the desk without moving a step. Why was she so frightened? It was absurd. Her father would be ashamed of her for being afraid of the dark. Giving herself a little impatient shake, she took two steps in front of her, groping with her hands like a blind person for obstacles in the way.

She stopped short and listened. Every nerve in her body was tingling and she felt she was trembling. For half a minute she hardly breathed. Then she resolutely began her march in the dark. At last the desk was reached and her hand was on the green china match holder. She stood for a moment irresolute. The pistol was in the lower left-hand desk drawer. She knew exactly where it was. Her father had shown it to her only the other day.

"I think you had better know where I keep it," he had said,

KATHERINE STOKES

"not that you will ever need to use it, I hope, because either Komatsu or I shall always be here to protect you, but just as a matter of precaution."

Again she reached for the match holder, but it was empty. Softly opening the drawer, she felt in the back until her fingers grasped the pistol. Carefully she drew it out and transferred it from her right hand to her left. There was an unacknowledged relief in Billie's heart that there were no matches. She felt she would rather get out of the library in the dark than make any investigations with a match. Once in the hall she would decide what to do.

She was morally certain now that someone else was in the room. She could see nothing, hear nothing, but in the dark she felt the presence of another human being. She recalled Nancy's experience.

"Perhaps it wasn't her imagination, after all," she thought.

The thing was to get back to the door and out of it. Billie wished with all her soul she had never come in at all. It had been a reckless, silly notion. Why should her father need a pistol? After all, it was just some roisterer on his way home from the festival. She had heard that *sake*, the Japanese brandy, made the men who drank it wild, no doubt wild enough to shoot off a pistol in the suburbs where there were no policemen about to interfere.

And all because she had heard this pistol shot, she had obeyed a foolish impulse to find her father's pistol. How reckless! How foolhardy! How stupid! Because, to come right down to a fine point, here she was shut up in a perfectly huge room, as black as the pit, with - someone else!

Never in all her experience had Billie been so frightened. Her knees knocked together and her head was quite giddy as she made her way unsteadily toward the door, still with the pistol in her left hand.

But she seemed to have lost all sense of direction. Groping with her right hand, she encountered a chair. There had been no chairs in the way before, - was it an hour ago or only a minute?

It would be better to get to the wall and feel her way along the shelves until she reached the door.

Why was she so panic-stricken? After all was she so sure about that other person crouching somewhere - anywhere?

Then the thing happened that she had known was going to happen all the time.

Reaching out in the dark, she encountered an arm. Instantly her right hand was seized in a grip of steel. There was a struggle. She was thrown to the floor; a shot; a cry - was it her own or another person's voice? Then absolute silence.

When Billie came back to consciousness, she was lying on a couch in the library. Miss Helen was kneeling beside her with the smelling salts. Mary was bathing her forehead with cold water and her father was chafing her wrists and saying in a low voice:

"You are not hurt, are you, Billie-girl? There, speak to father. Are you all right?"

There seemed to be a great many other people scattered about the room, the guests and the servants and her own particular friends leaning over her anxiously.

"I hope I didn't kill him?" she said weakly.

Mr. Campbell could not refrain from smiling.

"You are just a little girl after all, Billie," he said. "No, you didn't kill him, but you hit him. Look at that." He pointed to some blood spots on the rug. "You certainly winged him, whoever he was. In some way, he escaped. I don't know how, because we were in the hall when the shot was fired and the windows are still locked. He may have got out through the servants' quarters but that would have been difficult, too, without being seen."

Billie sat up.

"I'm all right now," she said. "It was only fright because I lost my way in the dark and couldn't find the door, and it was so ghastly running into another person in the blackness like that. Father, I wish you would tell them not to put out the lights in this room so early. It's the second time it's happened now."

"O'Haru, you hear what the lady says," said Mr. Campbell half humorously.

Billie, knowing her father as she did, was suddenly aware that he was trying to make light of the affair for the benefit of the others in the room. That the episode was far more serious than he cared to admit, she knew perfectly well.

O'Haru left the doorway where she had been standing and came over to the group by the couch.

"What was the honorable wish of the young lady?"

"Not to have the lights in the library put out so early in the evening. To wait until bedtime at least."

O'Haru disliked to contradict, but the august young lady was honorably mistaken. The lights had never been put out by any servant attached to the household. She herself, or her daughter, attended to that after the honorable family had retired for the night.

"Never mind," said Mr. Campbell in a soothing voice, indicating to Billie by a slight shake of the head that he would be glad if she would let the matter drop. Billie nodded. There was perfect understanding between the father and the daughter.

"How do you feel now, Miss Billie?" asked Nicholas Grimm coming to the foot of the couch.

"I'm all right again. I am ashamed of having been such a coward. If it had been daylight I shouldn't have been half so frightened."

"I feel that it was all my fault for running off and leaving you alone. I should have seen you to the house at least."

"Nonsense," said Billie. "That wouldn't have altered matters in the least. I would have come back here just the same for the pistol. You see I had a feeling that Papa might need it. Besides, we were all alone here. There were no men -"

"I am only glad it was someone else that was shot and not you, my darling child," broke in Miss Campbell tremulously. "Duncan, I do wish you wouldn't keep pistols lying around the house. They are so dangerous."

"But I don't, Cousin. It was carefully stored in the back compartment of a bottom desk drawer. If this reckless young relative of ours would go and dig it out, I'm sure it's not my fault."

"I'm sure I can't imagine why you treat the matter as such a joke," Miss Campbell was saying, when Mme. Fontaine swept into the room.

Her face was whiter than the long white wrap that enveloped her.

"I am so glad you were not injured," she said standing beside Billie.

"You must thank Mme. Fontaine, Billie. It was she who found you first. The rest of us were not certain in which room the shot was fired. I thought it was in the kitchen."

"Oh," said Billie, turning to the widow. "Were you the first person on the scene? You couldn't have seen much, it was so dark. How did you know I was here? I don't suppose the robber made any noise."

"It was very dark. I should not have known, if - if I had not smelt the smoke of the powder."

"I thought perhaps you were going to say you heard the robber groan," went on Billie. "You see I hit him. I think I must have a pretty good natural aim to shoot with the left hand in the dark and not fire wide of the mark. But I don't think he was very badly hurt. He got away so fast. I just winged him, I suppose."

"How do you know you shot him?" asked Mme. Fontaine.

Miss Helen pointed dramatically to the blood stains on the floor.

Suddenly the widow's lips turned quite white and a blue line appeared around her mouth. She swayed slightly and Mr. Campbell caught her. Billie was on her feet in a moment and they laid her on the couch.

"Unfasten her wrap," ordered Miss Campbell.

"No, no," said Mme. Fontaine in a very weak, thin voice. "The sight of blood -" she closed her eyes. "I shall be all right in a moment." Beads of perspiration appeared on her forehead and she shivered with a chill.

"I think Mme. Fontaine had better stay here to-night. She's too ill to get back to town," said Mr. Campbell.

"Oh, do," echoed the girls, and Miss Campbell added hospitably:

"We shall be so glad."

"I am quite well now," said the widow rising unsteadily to her feet. "You will forgive me, I hope. It is a faintness that comes to me at the sight of blood. Will you call my 'riksha now, Mr. Campbell? I must be going. I won't try to shake hands," she added, reaching the door. "I am still so light in the head, I am afraid of the effort. But I want to thank you for a delightful evening. I am only sorry it ended so disastrously."

Making a ceremonious Oriental bow to Miss Campbell and smiling and nodding to the others, she left the room followed by Mr. Campbell and the four girls.

"No one has told me yet what the shots were in the garden," announced Billie after the widow had departed.

"There was nothing to tell. We never found anything at all," answered Nicholas.

The next morning Mr. Campbell engaged another night watchman. His duty was to patrol the inside of the house, making his rounds every hour through the halls and living rooms. Between times he sat in the library.

CHAPTER XL

THE COMET DISGUISED.

"Where is Onoye, O'Haru?" Miss Campbell asked, a few days after the excitement in the library.

"Honorable Madam, Onoye much business."

To Miss Campbell, a seasoned housekeeper, this reply seemed a little irregular.

"What kind of business, O'Haru?" she demanded rather severely.

O'Haru looked amiably sad. It is true that Onoye was on the pay roll of the household servants, but then, did not her mother do work for two when Onoye was not actively engaged? The Japanese reasons thus: if the work is done properly, it is of no consequence who does it. Certainly the machinery of the household moved on without a hitch. There was no cause for complaint, but it seemed to Miss Campbell that if Onoye received wages she should appear about the house. Her position, which was practically that of ladies' maid, had been filled by one of the other small maids while O'Haru had covered up that vacancy by her own redoubled labors.

"Will you send Onoye to me, please," ordered Miss Campbell. "I have some sewing for her to do."

Poor O'Haru bowed. Her face looked wan and sad and it

seemed to the Motor Maids that Miss Campbell might not have been so severe; but as a housekeeper, that small, gentle lady was a disciplinarian.

They waited with some curiosity for Onoye to appear. In five minutes O'Sudzu, one of the other maids, stood framed in the doorway like a Japanese souvenir post card life size. She bowed low and entered the room timidly.

"But I sent for Onoye," exclaimed Miss Campbell.

O'Sudzu only smiled. She spoke no English.

"Onoye. Wish Onoye," repeated Miss Campbell. She pointed to the door.

O'Sudzu departed.

O'Matsu appeared next, and after O'Matsu came O'Kiku, who was followed presently by Masako, until these successive apparitions of Japanese maids became positively bewildering. The girls were consumed with the giggles and Miss Campbell was scarcely able to maintain a serious expression.

"No, no!" she would say each time, "Onoye! Wish Onoye!"

At last O'Haru appeared once more.

"August one, much kindness bestow. O'Haru make sewing."

"Where is Onoye? Where is your daughter?" demanded Miss Campbell.

O'Haru on her knees hung her head humbly.

"I think I know what's the matter," put in Mary. "Onoye is ill. I am sure it must be that."

"Is there anything the matter with Onoye?" asked Miss .

Campbell, but apparently O'Haru's English did not extend so far.

"Much sickness?" asked Billie.

O'Haru's head sank lower and lower.

"Poor thing," exclaimed Mary. "Onoye is ill, Miss Campbell, and O'Haru is afraid to say so."

"You must not be afraid, O'Haru. If little daughter ill, we take care of her. Bring doctor. See?"

"No, no, Onoye better. Onoye soon well," said the woman in a low voice. "Ask much pardons, gracious lady."

"Can't we see her?" asked Billie.

"Onoye see no one. Onoye only humble servant"

"Nonsense, she might be very ill," put in Miss Campbell. "I'll go with you now, O'Haru. Lead the way."

The housekeeper gave a sigh of patient resignation and rose to her feet. Miss Campbell and the girls followed her down the long hall and across the passage to the servants' quarters.

At last they came to a small room at the end of the house. The floor was covered with the usual wicker mats. The *shoji*, or sliding partitions, were drawn together, and in the dim mellow light which filtered through these opaque walls they saw Onoye. She was stretched on the mat which is the usual Japanese bed, her neck on the uncomfortable little pillow bench. With a murmur of surprise and apology, she pulled herself weakly to her knees and touched her forehead to the floor.

"Pardon, gracious lady," she said, drawing her kimono closely about her.

"But, child, we didn't know you were so ill," said Miss Campbell, gently forcing the girl to lie down on her bed. "Has the doctor seen you?"

"Yes, gracious lady"

"What is the matter with you?"

Onoye shook her head.

"Not say it in English." She touched her forehead. "Muchly fire."

"It's fever, of course," said Miss Campbell, kneeling beside the sick girl and feeling her forehead. "I think you had better not stay here, children. It might be something contagious."

"Nonsense," thought Billie; but Miss Campbell was in one of her compelling humors and they retreated obediently, leaving her to hold a conference with O'Haru and to see that everything was done that could be done to alleviate Onoye's sufferings. She finally departed, after satisfying herself that Onoye was in the toils of a bilious attack. But she did not administer calomel as she would have done in ordinary cases of torpid liver. "I suppose the doctor knows what he is about," she said, "and there must be a Japanese equivalent to calomel in a country where it rains eternally."

It was decided that they should take the "Comet" out after lunch. Miss Campbell wished to visit an apothecary shop and there were other plans for sight-seeing, - perhaps the magnificent Shiba Temple and the wisteria in the park. But before they were to go, there were two surprises in store, one for Billie alone and one for all of them. Just after luncheon while the others were dressing for the trip, Billie, who needed about two minutes for pinning on her hat and slipping on her coat, went back to the stable to take the "Comet" from his garage. On the way, she passed the room occupied by O'Haru and her daughter. Not having the least fear of contagion, she entered a back passage of the intricate house, which reminded her of the houses she used to build with cards as a child. Pushing back the partition she marched into Onoye's room without announcing herself.

"There's nothing to knock on, so why knock?" she thought.

Billie surprised the little Japanese girl sitting up examining her arm, which was wrapped in bandages.

"Why, Onoye, I didn't know you had been injured," she exclaimed, running over and kneeling beside the sick girl.

Onoye was speechless. She tried to cover her arm with the sleeve of her kimono and to apologize and bow all at the same time.

"Not muchly badly," she said at last in a low voice.

"But how did it happen?"

"Not nothing. Pardon grant," murmured Onoye.

"Of course, you poor dear, but how did you injure yourself?"

She laid the bandaged wrist gently on the palm of her hand and looked at it.

"Poor small accident," said Onoye.

"But why was it?"

The two girls looked at each other silently.

"Was it in the library that night?" asked Billie after a long pause.

Onoye's head drooped more and more.

"Poor little thing. Poor child," exclaimed Billie, consumed with pity and remorse, since it had been her own carelessness that had caused the poor small accident.

Onoye had doubtless put out the lights and when she, Billie, had crept into the room like a thief, the Japanese girl was frightened and hid herself behind a chair. Then when they had collided, they had both lost their heads and the pistol had gone off. In spite of her remorse, Billie was immensely relieved.

"Papa will be, too," she thought. "It had much better be Onoye than a robber."

And Mr. Campbell was decidedly relieved when he heard the story from his daughter that night.

"I'll keep it a secret, Onoye, dear," said Billie, moved by compassion. "I'll only tell Papa. I am so sorry I shot you. It must have hurt terribly."

Onoye tried to smile.

"Forgiveness grant," she murmured again.

"I think I'd better say 'forgiveness grant,'" said Billie. "But I must be going now." She patted Onoye on the cheek and then tiptoed out of the room. "It is a relief," she thought, turning her footsteps toward the garage.

Some minutes later, Billie ran into her cousin's room breathlessly.

"Ready in one moment," called Miss Campbell, who had heard the whir of the motor at the door.

"I want to prepare you for a surprise," said Billie solemnly. "I don't mind telling you that I have had the shock of my life."

"But what is it?" they all demanded in one voice.

"I'll only say this much. Papa has punished the 'Comet' for running over the child that day."

"How?"

"You'll see. I thought I had better prepare you. The shock might have killed you if I hadn't."

"Goodness gracious me, what is it?" cried Miss Campbell, seizing her reticule and gloves and rushing into the hall, followed by the others.

When she reached the piazza, she sat down flat in a chair and gasped.

There was the "Comet," to be sure. His outlines were as familiar as the profile of a beloved brother, but his beautiful scarlet coat had been taken from him and he wore instead a quiet covering of dark blue. The luxurious red cushions were covered with buff linen. One small decoration had been conceded by Mr. Campbell. The dark, quietly colored coat was relieved on each side by the buff-colored initials, "M-M" lovingly intertwined.

"I suppose Papa thought the red coat was too gaudy," said Billie, who was indeed just a little tearful over the loss of that cheerful and familiar scarlet dress which would never again flash along the highways like a scarlet bird. "But he's the same old 'Comet' inside," she added hastily. "You couldn't change his noble disposition if you painted him sea green."

"I think he looks beautiful," put in Elinor. "He's so neat and elegant in buff and blue. It's like a livery."

The other girls laughed because Elinor's speech was so characteristic.

"Oh, you regal young person," exclaimed Nancy. "Your imagination doesn't stop at anything short of liveried retinues of servants. There is no doubt you were a royal princess in a previous existence. And suppose you are a fat old pug in another life, like Nedda!"

"I am sure Nedda is waited on hand and foot," cried Elinor. "She has a maid who follows her around with a cushion and a silk cover."

Komatsu, standing at the side of the motor, grinned with amusement.

"They are foolish children, aren't they, Komatsu?" observed Miss Campbell, climbing into her accustomed seat.

Nedda, hearing her name mentioned, wobbled on her uncertain old legs to the edge of the piazza and whined piteously.

"Go back to your mat, you pathetic, pampered old great grandmother," called Nancy.

The aged animal turned obediently and curled herself on her cushion. Then she lifted her wrinkled, snub-nosed face to watch the departing motorists.

"She does look like our Irish cook's grandmother," said Nancy.

Everybody laughed gaily and the feelings regarding the "Comet's" new blue coat were dispelled. Nedda had been a welcome interruption.

"Papa always does the right thing," Billie announced presently. "I'm glad he did it now. I was a little hurt at first, of course. But I understand perfectly what his reasons were. Everybody will be looking out for a red motor car that runs over people and they'll never recognize the 'Comet' It's just as if he wore a disguise."

The dark blue car was, as a matter of fact, not nearly so

conspicuous as he skimmed along over the road, and it was the very wisest thing Billie's father could have done to change the color. Probably every man, woman and child in the multitude that had clustered around the car that day on Arakawa Ridge would be constantly on the look-out for the red machine, and never glance twice at the blue one.

"I do feel so inconspicuous and quiet and lady-like," remarked Billie when some time later they left the motor car in charge of Komatsu and went in to visit Shiba Temple in Shiba Park. These chapels are mostly the tombs of the Shoguns who for many years were powerful nobles and who really ruled Japan in place of the Emperor, a mere figurehead in those days. The magnificent tombs they built for themselves are now the very pride of Tokyo. Within the great red gates of the main temple, upheld with scarlet columns, wheeled flights of pigeons quite tame. The girls bought packages of grain from little booths and fed them and presently one of the pretty creatures perched on Mary's wrist and ate from her hand.

"Don't frighten him," she whispered, her eyes brimming with tears of pleasure.

All the afternoon the tourists wandered through the wide courts where were armies of stone lanterns placed in exactly the right spots. They passed softly flowing fountains wherein the worshippers washed themselves and climbed stately stairs by fern-set walls. Court within court they entered adorned with magnificent paintings and carvings of marvelous workman-ship. They walked through the great hall of books where scrolls of immense value are kept, each swathed in silk and lying in its own lacquer box. At last dazzled and silenced by the succession of magic courts, they returned to the outer world of the living, and climbed into the motor car.

"Before we go home, don't you think we had better inquire for Mme.

Fontaine?" Billie suggested.

Miss Campbell assented. So long as they did not go in, she was quite willing.

They found the gate of the Widow of Shanghai's garden stretched wide open; a jinriksha was about to pass into the street. A Japanese lady in a rich costume was the occupant. She exchanged one swift glance with Billie and quickly looked the other way. Billie started slightly. She felt uncomfortable. It seemed to her that she had been looking straight into the eyes of Mme. Fontaine.

"Did you notice," said Mary, "that the Japanese lady in the 'riksha wore her arm in a sling?"

No, they had not noticed it, but there was nothing remarkable in that. No one even commented on the fact, while they waited for Komatsu to inquire and leave their cards.

"Mme. Fontaine was still very much indisposed," the message came back, "but she would be glad if the ladies would enter and have some refreshment. She regretted she would not be able to see them herself."

The ladies would not enter, however, as it was nearing the hour when Mr. Campbell would return and expect to find them in the garden waiting tea, and the "Comet" bore them swiftly home.

CHAPTER XII.

A THEATER PARTY.

"It's very easy for a bachelor to entertain in Japan," remarked Mr. Buxton one afternoon in the Campbells' summer house. "A busy man is saved all bother and inconvenience if he wants to give a theater party, say, with a dinner to follow, by putting the affair in the hands of an 'elder sister,'"

"Suppose he hasn't any elder sister," put in Miss Campbell feeling slightly offended. Perhaps she was older than Mr. Buxton, but she was sure she didn't look it and she had no intention of being designated as his "elder sister."

"Oh, but he always has," replied Mr. Buxton. "A Japanese providence always provides a *Nesan*, or elder sister, for persons desiring to entertain. All she requires of you is to leave her alone and pay the bill."

Miss Campbell felt somewhat mollified.

"But what does she do?" asked Mary.

"She does all the work, makes all the arrangements, engages the boxes and the 'rikshas, orders the dinner, tells you how to act; in fact, does everything any good elder sister would do to oblige a little brother."

The others smiled at this droll notion but there was something rather touching, too, about the simple title of elder sister or *Nesan* for this efficient and reliable individual who took all the burdens on her own shoulders. As a matter of fact a *Nesan* is the proprietor of a tea house and her business is to get up entertainments.

"And it is for this reason," continued Mr. Buxton, "that I am able to ask all of you for the honor of your company to the theater to-morrow at three and later to dinner. I could never have undertaken it alone, but having been provided with an efficient relative older and wiser than I am, although she looks to be under thirty, I feel no uneasiness whatever."

"I am inclined to accept your reluctant invitation on the spot, Buxton," laughed Mr. Campbell, "for self and family."

"I didn't intend it to appear reluctant," answered the Englishman. "I only wanted to assure you that if you would do me the honor of coming to the entertainment, all things would be correctly carried out according to Japanese etiquette and there would not be a hitch in the whole affair. Will you come?"

"We shall be delighted, Mr. Buxton," answered Miss Campbell.

"I thought you would," he added. "Indeed, I was so certain of it that the little *Nesan* has already got a list of the guests and the whole thing has been arranged."

"And to make assurance doubly sure, you thought you would just mention the matter to us?" asked Mr. Campbell, who enjoyed teasing this rather odd and amusing old bachelor.

"How do we dress?" asked Nancy.

"I never thought to ask the *Nesan* how the ladies should dress. But if you take my advice, I should say comfortably. That is, if you can. I believe a woman's clothes are never really comfortable."

"Mine are," broke in Billie, poised on the railing of the summer house swinging her feet carelessly.

"Would you have us dress like men?" demanded Miss Campbell indignantly.

"No indeed, Madam," answered the bachelor, "but in your present costume, you must admit that it would be difficult to sit on the floor."

"But I don't wish to sit on the floor," exclaimed the spinster. "It's a perfectly absurd custom. Besides, you are edging away from the main point - trying to draw out of the -"

"There will be no chairs to-morrow," interrupted the other, blinking his eyes like a wise old bird. "And," he continued as he took his departure, "neither will there be any knives and forks."

"I shall take mine along, then," called Miss Campbell, whose discussions with the bachelor kept them in a constant state of amusement.

"It would be an unpardonable breach of etiquette," he called over his shoulder. Presently he turned back and added, "You are not to use that infernal machine for my party. The *Nesan* provided 'rikshas for all guests."

"But that's just an additional expense to you, Buxton," cried Mr. Campbell.

"I know it perfectly well and I so suggested to my elder sister, but she didn't seem to understand, and I decided I would rather hire a gross of 'rikshas than try and make her. So you may expect three of 'em to-morrow at a quarter past two. The performance begins at three."

"Dear old 'Comet,' he's always getting slighted nowadays," remarked Billie. "He never gets to go anywhere."

"He's probably glad enough to sit in his cell and meditate on the mutability of human events," answered Mr. Buxton, and this time he really did go.

It happened therefore that the "Comet" was once more left in humiliating retirement while his young mistresses rode off in jinrikshas which appeared at the door exactly at the hour mentioned by the host of the afternoon. Indeed the motor car had good reason to be a disgruntled machine. He never did seem to be a part of the Japanese landscape like the graceful 'riksha. As a matter of fact he was a blot on the scene and entirely out of place against a background of an ancient temple or a group of picturesque individuals in clothes more brilliant in hue than his own boyhood coat.

Converging from various points in Tokyo but all timed to meet at the theater door exactly at five minutes to three, came the other guests of the party in 'rikshas provided by the *Nesan*. Mme. Fontaine was one of these.

"What a picture she is," exclaimed Nancy, noticing at once the widow's beautiful costume of embroidered pongee over which she wore a kimono-shaped mantle of the same embroidered silk, the sleeves of which covered her arms and hands completely.

Nodding and smiling at the girls brightly, she followed Miss Campbell into the theater where they were met by the plump, hospitable little *Nesan*, who prostrated herself before each guest and removed shoes at the same time.

Miss Campbell groaned.

"Oh, dear," she complained. "Even at the theater! I shall never get accustomed to walking flat-footed. I shall be wearing bifurcated stockings next, I suppose."

"Etiquette, Madam, etiquette," said Mr. Buxton. "You must do as the Romans do, remember, or else be thought extremely rude."

But there was no time for argument and the party hastily distributed themselves in the two boxes. Yoritomo Ito kept close beside Nancy while Nicholas Grimm and Reggie Carlton sat tailor fashion in the back of the box. The theater was a strange place to the Western eye. There was not a chair in the entire house and Mr. Buxton chuckled aloud over Miss Campbell's complaints when she was obliged to sit on a mat on the floor. Below the two tiers of boxes, the pit appeared like a gigantic checker-board divided into square compartments by partitions about a foot high. In each compartment squatted six people. Running from the rear of the house to the stage was a slightly raised walk three feet broad to be used by the actors as an exit. The stalls were crowded with men and women and children. Here and there were groups of geishas or dancing girls. Their rich apparel made bright spots of color in the scene. The children ran about with perfect freedom, up and down the aisles at the sides and in and out of the stalls, eating sweetmeats and visiting their friends. And there was scarcely a grown person in the entire audience of Japanese who was not smoking, for women as well as men smoke in Japan: one pinch of tobacco in a short pipe, one puff, a little whiff of smoke inhaled and the operation is over. Before the curtain rose, the *Nesan* flew busily from one box to the other with cushions and sweetmeats, baskets of oranges and boxes of sweet pickled black beans. Presently came the sound of two blocks of wood striking together. Then the curtain rose and the audience settled itself for three hours of the most intense enjoyment. The play was a Japanese legend and the actors picturesque and dramatic, but if all the greatest actors in the world had combined to give the performance, Miss Campbell could not have maintained her cramped position a minute longer than two hours.

"I am sure my limbs will refuse their office, Duncan," she whispered. "If this goes on much longer, I shall have to be carried from the theater like a helpless paralytic."

"Buxton, don't you think we've had enough?" suggested Mr. Campbell, and the bachelor, glad to stretch his own cramped legs, took the hint and gave the signal for departure.

Once more they were in the 'rikshas, only this time Nancy found herself seated by Yoritomo and Billie and Nicholas had paired off in the same way. Miss Campbell was not sure that she approved of this change.

"In my day," she remarked to her cousin, "young ladies never rode alone in buggies with young men."

"But they aren't buggies, Cousin," he answered good-naturedly.

"They are, all but the horse," said Miss Campbell.

But they had arrived at the gate of the tea house before the argument could proceed and were presently rolling through a garden enclosed by high walls. It was a fairyland of a place, even more beautiful than the Campbells' own garden, filled with brilliant beds of flowers and here and there a small grove of stunted pine trees.

Through the door of a tea house, low roofed and brown (houses are not painted in Japan), rushed a score of *musumes* (maids), pink-cheeked and bare-footed, who greeted the guests with low bows and removed their shoes. There also was their own particular *Nesan*, owner of that particular tea house, who bowed gracefully and said in Japanese:

"Be honorably pleased to enter."

Inside, the tea house was scrupulously clean. The bare boards in the hall seemed worn thin by scrubbing and nowhere were any furniture or ornaments except the hanging scroll. The floors were covered with soft wicker mats and presently they were all seated in a semicircle at one end of the room. The younger members of the party were in a perfect gale of subdued laughter by this time. Elinor, too dignified to look where she was going, had stubbed her august toe and for at least half a minute had hopped on one foot in an agony of pain. Nicholas had privately circulated a rumor that live carp would be one of the courses, and not to eat a small piece would give grievous offense to the *Nesan* and her *musumes*.

After a little table about a foot high had been placed before each guest, a procession of miniature waitresses entered with the dinner. In quick succession were served fish soup, crushed birds with sugared walnuts and oranges, broiled fish with tiny balls of sweetened potatoes, and numerous other strange but not unpalatable dishes, and all the while streams of hors d'ouvres: horseradish, spinach and seaweed. But they were not obliged to eat with chop sticks. Mr. Buxton had provided knives and forks.

At last with the greatest ceremony, the little proprietor herself appeared bearing a large silver tray.

"Here it comes," whispered Nicholas. "What did I tell you?"

There, sure enough, was the carp, taken from the water a moment before and sliced into delicate pink steaks. He lay on a bed of fresh water grasses and leaves, and each portion was served in a dainty mat of twisted grass. Nobody refused a sacrificial morsel, but only Yoritomo and Mr. Buxton had the courage to eat it. Mr. Buxton swallowed his at a gulp and Miss Campbell shivered all over at the sight.

"How could you?" she exclaimed in a whisper.

"Etiquette," he answered. "I would swallow a mouse for the sake of etiquette in this polite country."

During the dinner there had been a sound of suppressed laughter and the tinkle of music behind the partitions, and now, after the last round of the innumerable courses had been served, the partitions were shoved aside and four samisen players entered followed by eight dancing girls. Nothing could equal the grace of their bows as they glided softly in. Their smiles of welcome were inimitable. Then their faces became grave and serious and the dance began. The oldest was hardly more than fifteen and the youngest about ten. They were like sober-faced little dolls in gorgeous brocaded robes as they paraded, stamped their white-stockinged feet and postured with elaborate fans.

Mme. Fontaine, who had eaten no dinner and talked very little, watched the dancers with intense interest.

"Are they not charming little creatures?" she asked Mr. Campbell. "They are trained to be so, - to sing, dance and amuse and to look pretty. But I assure you some of them develop into splendid women. Many of them marry well. The geisha girl is not always a butterfly."

There was a subdued fire in her eyes as she spoke.

Mr. Campbell looked at her curiously.

"You have a special tenderness for them, I see," he remarked.

"I was one," she said.

While this little colloquy was going on, Yoritomo was whispering into Nancy's ear:

"You think they are pretty? But they are not so beautiful as you. There are no blue eyes in Japan."

And Nicholas was saying to Billie:

"By Jove, it's terrible sitting in this position for three hours at a stretch. Do you think we could slip into the garden? I have something I want to tell you."

Being on the end of the semi-circle, they crept behind one of the sliding partitions and rose stiffly to their feet. Two steps more and they were in the garden, now flooded with moonlight.

"It's romantic," observed Billie, "but what will Cousin Helen say? She's a very strict chaperone."

"Tell her you couldn't endure it another moment; or tell her I couldn't, which would be perfectly true. I feel as if I had shrunk a few inches. I can't stand up straight."

Turning down a walk leading to the little gold fish pond, they presently paused on the miniature bridge and looked down at the reflections of the stars mirrored in the pool beneath. They were quite silent for a moment. Then Nicholas cleared his throat and began in an embarrassed and hesitating way:

"Miss Billie, can you keep a secret?"

"Don't you think that is rather an uncomplimentary question?" answered Billie. "I must have made a poor impression on you."

"Indeed you haven't. You have made just the other kind," he replied with boyish candor. "That's why I wanted to tell you something, but it was a stupid way to begin. Please forgive me. Of course you can keep a secret. Any girl who is cool-headed enough to run a motor car and - and keep machinery in order and -"

"Well - and what?"

"I think you are just great, Miss Billie. I never met a girl like you before," he mumbled half audibly. "That's why I wanted to tell you something - that is - confide something to you."

Billie looked uncomfortable. She was only a month younger than Nancy, but she Was far less experienced in the ways of the world, her tastes being more boyish and simple than those of that gay little coquette.

"In the first place, you knew I was a civil engineer. That's how I happened to meet your father. Every engineer in the country wanted to meet him, because he is a very famous one himself, as you probably know."

Billie was pleased at this compliment. Her father was too modest to tell such things about himself, and she had no way of knowing his reputation unless other people told her.

"It was through Yoritomo that I came to Japan. We were friends in New York; and it was through his uncle, who is high up in public affairs here, that I got an appointment almost immediately. It's been interesting work, most of the time around Tokyo, and I have enjoyed the experience. But, you see, I came here with just a little money and fell on my feet and feel that I am under obligations to Yoritomo and his family for a good many favors."

"Of course," answered Billie. "But what of it?"

"Well," began Nicholas slowly, "Yoritomo has been a good friend to me. I have always liked him and looked up to him because he's a deal cleverer than I am and a wonderful student, - but lately, - it's hard to explain to you, Miss Bille, but I -"

"Don't you like him any more?"

"No, no, it isn't that." Nicholas paused again and wiped beads of perspiration from his face. He shifted his position and dug his hands into his pockets. "I don't think I can say it," he said. "I thought I could, but it's too deuced hard."

"Go on, you silly boy."

"Well, to tell you the truth, I don't trust him," he blurted out.

"But Papa likes him," said Billie, simply, feeling that her

father's sanction was as good as a royal stamp of approval.

"Oh, yes, of course. Everybody likes him. It isn't that."

"Then what are you driving at?"

"Good heavens, I don't know what I am driving at. Only, you see, I introduced Yoritomo to the family and something happened the other day that made me uneasy. It seemed to me that I ought to warn you not to get too thick with him - that is - not you but Miss Brown. You see, Japanese are different - they take things more seriously -" Nicholas plunged deeper and deeper in.

"Can't you tell me what happened?"

"That's the queer part. There's nothing really to tell. It was one of those little incidents that mean everything or nothing. I couldn't tell Mr. Campbell because it was too insignificant, but I thought I might make a clean breast of it to you and you could warn Miss Brown - well - not to talk too much to Yoritomo. She might tell him something -"

"But Nancy hasn't any secrets to tell, Mr. Grimm."

"I thought you promised to call me Nicholas? I didn't say she had, but these Japanese are the wiliest people. They will use you without your knowing you are being used. Couldn't you just tell Miss Nancy to be careful without explaining why? Don't girls ever do that? Just say that Yoritomo's a Jap, and Japs are deep people and she had better not tell him all she knows."

Billie laughed.

"Why, yes, I could, I suppose, but I'm sure it's not necessary. She doesn't know anything to tell."

"Whew!" ejaculated Nicholas, fanning himself with his hat.

"I'd rather dig a tunnel through a mountain than have to do that again. I decided I had to do it and I have been working it over in my mind for days. First I thought of Miss Campbell, but she would have gone off her head about it. Miss Brown wouldn't have understood, either. She would have been angry, I suppose. So I decided to come to you. I felt sure you would understand and know exactly what to do."

Billie smiled. She was beginning to be very fond of this boyish, honest young man whose nature was not unlike her own. Just at that moment they saw Yoritomo and Nancy strolling along a moonlit path. He was talking to her in a low intense voice and she was smiling and dimpling as usual. It occurred to Billie that Nancy was getting very grown up all of a sudden and for her part, she couldn't see any fun in it at all. She had noticed lately that Nancy did not enjoy their old-time girlish fun half so much as she used to. She would rather stroll in the garden with a young man than with her four devoted friends, and "hen parties" as she called them, did not amuse her any longer.

Billie began to feel quite serious about the benighted state of her best friend. Her nature was deeply tinged with sympathy and sweetness, but she was not yet old enough to feel tolerant with Nancy for growing up and craving beaux and flattery.

"I will speak to Nancy Brown," she thought, and that night going home in the 'riksha by Nancy's side she turned the matter over in her mind. "But not to-night," she decided, for Nancy had never seemed more adorable than on that ride, chatting with her friend about the evening's pleasures.

CHAPTER XIII.

A FALLING OUT.

Several days went swiftly by and still Billie had not delivered the warning to her beloved Nancy.

After all, was it really necessary to warn Nancy not to talk too much and tell all she knew? That was a man's idea of a girl's conversation: to tell all she knew. How absurd! Besides, Nancy was not much of a conversationalist and it's only people who talk all the time who tell secrets. After they exhaust every other subject, they begin to draw on their confidential stock.

The more Billie turned the question over in her mind, the more far-fetched it seemed, and at last she determined not to mention it at all.

"Who am I to be scolding anybody?" she said to herself. "I am sure I am far from perfect and it would look rather presumptuous to criticize Nancy who hasn't done anything to be criticized for."

But these noble and modest sentiments were not destined to remain unchanged in Billie's mind. By a curious chain of circumstances, the very thing she had concluded to avoid was brought about.

The circumstances began in the morning before breakfast and led up, one after another, to the first real quarrel the two friends had ever had since their friendship began.

It had been raining all night, a hot sticky downpour, and nobody in the house had slept well. The atmosphere was oppressive, and breathing became a conscious effort; so that the American members of the household were fretful and out of humor after a disagreeable and restless night. Even the most even-tempered and well-balanced natures are upset by a steaming, humid temperature which seems to creep into the soul and enshroud the brighter self with mist.

Billie felt the general depression and after breakfast she followed her friends in a disconsolate procession to the library.

"There are as many different kinds of rain as there are people," she observed. "The rain in Scotland was like a brisk scolding person. At least there was nothing monotonous and tiring about it. It had plenty of vigor and energy. But this Japanese summer rain is like a great, fat, stupid, lazy creature who never lifts a little finger to do anything but just rain and rain and turn into misty steam!"

"One hasn't even the energy to read a book," sighed Mary.

"As Reggie Carlton says, 'it's so infernally damp,'" put in Elinor, and the others smiled languidly. Elinor was indeed feeling the humidity to quote a semi-profane expression.

Nancy was really the most cheerful member of the party. She had an air of expecting something which appeared to give her a reason for existing.

After the outbursts of her three friends, there was a long and heavy silence broken only by the steady patter of the rain on the roof.

At last Nancy rose and smiling mysteriously, said:

"Excuse me, ladies. While your company is highly exciting, I must leave you to write letters."

"I can't imagine to whom," exclaimed Billie.

"I mailed four for you yesterday to your mother and father and 'Merry' and Percy St. Clair."

Billie knew Nancy's affairs quite as well as she knew her own; two sisters could hardly have been more intimately associated.

"Guess again, Miss Inquisitive," said Nancy. "And guess fifty times more if you like. You'll never guess the right person and I shan't tell you for punishment. So there!"

For some reason - of course it was the weather - Billie felt teased and hurt. Not for anything would she have kept Nancy in ignorance of any of her correspondence.

"I didn't mean to be inquisitive." she called, half apologe- tically. "I was merely surprised at your being so mysterious."

"When you get to be as old as I am," said Nancy in a lofty tone, "you'll know better than to tell all you know."

"I'll never get to be as old as you are, Miss Nancy-Bell," retorted Billie. "It's a physical impossibility, since you are two months older than I am."

Nancy departed from the room, calling out laughingly:

"Smarty! Smarty!"

Billie kicked off her slipper after her, and so the quarrel started with good natured raillery. But the memory of the letter lingered in Billie's mind all the morning, although why it should have connected itself with Onoye, who, an hour later, stepped out into the garden on high wooden clogs with an oiled paper umbrella, she could not say. Standing idly by the window, Billie watched the little figure disappear down the path.

"I suppose she's going to visit the Compassionate God again," Billie thought to herself absently. "I hope he'll be compassionate enough to clear the weather by to-morrow."

The next link in the chain of circumstances was forged when Onoye returned from her pilgrimage. Billie, who had drawn a stool to the window and was sitting with her face pressed against the glass, saw her walking slowly along the dripping path to the house. The Japanese girl was looking at something she held in her free hand, an envelope undoubtedly. Just as she reached the piazza, Onoye slipped the letter into the folds of her sash and hurried in.

Billie's mind gave a sudden leap of conjecture but she continued to sit quietly, her face against the window, peering into the mist-hung garden.

"Funny," she said to herself. "It couldn't have been a Japanese letter because those are rolled up on little sticks."

Not long afterwards, she encountered Onoye in the passage. The Japanese girl smiled lovingly into her face. Little by little her feeling for Billie was growing and expanding into a real devotion,

"And I'm sure I don't know why she should caress the hand that smote her," Billie had thought. "She's a dear, faithful little soul."

"Are you quite well again, Onoye?" she asked, pausing and slipping her arm around the Japanese girl's shoulders.

"Yes, honorable lady. Not any sickly arm no more."

"And have you been writing a letter to thank the Compassionate God Jizu for your recovery?" went on Billie.

A frightened look came into Onoye's eyes. The English had been too much for her comprehension, but the word "letter" she had understood perfectly.

"No understand," she said, bowing ceremoniously. And she hastened away, leaving Billie much puzzled and rather curious, too.

The day dragged slowly on, and still the rain poured and the mist steamed and there was no relief from the circumstances of the weather. Miss Campbell had been feeling rheumatic twinges in her "old joints," as she called them, and remained in bed reading an agreeable novel. Once more the four friends retired to the library where Mary read aloud and the others engaged in various characteristic pursuits. Elinor was embroidering a royal coat-of-arms in colored silks on a cushion cover; Nancy was darning a rent in a lace flounce and Billie was darning her father's socks. This task she undertook each week with extraordinary cheerfulness, although Onoye had offered to do it for her, and O'Haru had almost taken the darning needle and egg from her by force.

As the hands of the clock neared four, Nancy rose.

"Go on with your reading, Mary," she said. "I need some more thread and I shall have to look for it. So don't wait."

"What number do you want?" asked Elinor.

Nancy looked annoyed.

"Oh, something quite fine. I know you haven't it, Elinor."

"Will a hundred do?" asked Elinor, extracting the spool from her neat sewing bag.

"That's too fine."

"I have all sizes here."

"Never mind," exclaimed Nancy impatiently, and hastened

from the room, taking her lace-flounced skirt with her.

"Stubborn person," observed Elinor and once more plunged into her aristocratic labors.

Billie grew more and more restless. The book Mary was reading aloud was a detective story, lately arrived from America. It had reached a thrilling point, but Billie could not fasten her attention.

"I think I'll just be obliged to get out and walk," she burst out unexpectedly. "I can't stand this life of inaction a minute longer. Don't stop reading on my account, Mary, dear. I don't suppose I could tempt either of you two hot-house plants to come with me, could I?"

"Since it's just as hot outside as inside, I don't think you could," answered Elinor.

"Perhaps Nancy will go," thought Billie, hastening down the long hall to their joint apartment.

But Nancy was not in the room. Her lace petticoat had been thrown hastily on the bed with her sewing box. Billie searched over the entire house for her friend without success.

"Funny," she thought, slipping on her over-shoes and raincoat and seizing an umbrella from the stand in the passage.

Presently she found herself in the mist-hung garden, and instinctively her steps turned toward the little bridge and the shrine to the Compassionate God. All the way, she kept thinking:

"What is Nancy-Bell up to? Not that, - surely. Why should she write letters that way? Nobody would object to their coming by mail. It's just her romantic notions," her thoughts continued as she reached the bridge.

Taking the curved path to the foot of the small embankment, the next moment Billie came full upon Nancy and Yoritomo Ito talking earnestly together. There was something rather amusing in their appearance, because down the ribs of their two umbrellas rivulets of water dripped and poured in streams about them.

"Oh, I beg your pardon," exclaimed Billie, the prey to varying emotions: embarrassment, hurt feelings, surprise and, it must be confessed, a dash of anger.

"Oh, Billie," said Nancy, starting violently, "how you frightened me."

"How do you do, Mr. Ito," said Billie stiffly.

"How do you do, Miss Campbell. We seem to be having several unexpected encounters this afternoon. Here was Miss Brown out for a wet stroll on a day when ladies usually remain indoors, and now you come, too. American young ladies are very athletic."

"It isn't a case of exercise with me, Mr. Ito. I came out really to find Nancy," said Billie coldly.

"I shall bid you good afternoon," answered Yoritomo in his most formal manner. "I was just taking a short cut. Pardon my trespassing on your grounds."

Billie detested untruths and she knew quite well that Yoritomo was not speaking the real truth. She looked at Nancy reproachfully.

"Good-bye," she said and turned her back.

Yoritomo made an elaborate bow and departed and Nancy followed Billie slowly up the dripping path. Half way back, Billie stopped short and wheeled around.

"I should think you'd be ashamed of yourself, Nancy Brown," she exclaimed.

Nancy had never seen Billie really angry before and she was frightened at the new hard look that had come into the frank gray eyes. But Nancy was in no mood to be scolded. The truth is, she had reached a difficult age and it was not going to be easy to manage her by lecturing and argument. She had an enormous appetite for flattery and the power of her prettiness had intoxicated her.

"Oh, I don't suppose you would understand, Billie, even if I tried to explain," she answered hotly. "I haven't done anything to be ashamed of."

"Meeting people in the garden secretly isn't anything to be proud of," pursued Billie. "And exchanging letters by a servant," she burst out suddenly recalling Onoye's unaccountable trip that morning an the rain. "I have been told to warn you not to talk too much to Mr. Ito. He's not to be trusted, and I think this a very good time to do it."

Nancy flushed. She was angrier than Billie now. The two girls had turned and were facing each other furiously. Billie felt the pulse leap in her temples and something gripped her throat. The sensation was so new to her that she scarcely knew how to handle it. It was like trying to rein in a runaway horse.

"He's just as nice as Nicholas Grimm," cried Nancy. "I should think you'd be ashamed to spy on anyone. I never thought it of you."

This statement was so unjust that Billie's rage leaped out of all bounds and got beyond her control entirely.

"That is untrue. I did not spy on you. I merely put two and two together and guessed the rest. Can you deny it? And do you call it lady-like and honorable? I don't. I call it common and horrid."

Billie's voice in her extreme anger was very stern. She carefully avoided calling Nancy by name. She felt if she spoke the name of her friend, she must cry and not for anything did she want to humble herself just then.

"I tell you I won't explain," ejaculated Nancy. "I've done nothing wrong and I think you are very hard and unjust. It's because you are still a child about some things, Billie. When you are older and have had more experience, you will learn not to be a prig."

Older and more experienced! Now all the saints defend us! Billie laughed bitterly. Both girls were on the point of weeping and perhaps, if their anger had changed to tears at that moment, much bitterness might have been saved them. But they were interrupted by Mr. Campbell, who now appeared, walking at a leisurely gait up the path.

"Well, well, children! Here is devotion indeed," he exclaimed when he espied his daughter and her friend standing stock still in the pouring rain. "So intimate and absorbed in each other's society that you are oblivious to the weather! That's the right kind of friendship. I would not have it any other way. How are you, little daughter?" he asked, kissing Billie and shaking hands with Nancy at the same time. "And how's little daughter's friend?"

Not for worlds would they have disclosed the real truth to Mr. Campbell. Billie drew her arm through her father's and Nancy followed them to the house.

"Do you think the rain will ever let up, Papa?" asked Billie, resting her cheek against her father's shoulder.

Nancy felt suddenly frightfully homesick for her own bluff good-natured parent.

"Well, it once rained forty days and forty nights, you know," said Mr. Campbell. "And what's happened before may happen again."

Habitual wranglers regard quarrels as mere ripples on the surface and soon forget about them, but the two girls were unaccustomed to such scenes and their feelings were deeply lacerated.

"Let not the sun go down upon your wrath," Billie thought, as she lay beside Nancy that night, but she remembered that Nancy had called her a spy and her soul was filled with bitterness.

CHAPTER XIV.

A LETTER THAT CAME
THOUGH IT WAS NEVER SENT.

The two girls put the width of the bed between them that night. Each lay stiffly on the very edge of the mattress and silently pondered over the situation. Anger was not a self-indulgence with either of them and the attack was so unusual that it left them both unnerved and shaken. Nancy had only played with her food at dinner and Billie, who had eaten without an appetite, now felt the discomfort of a burning indigestion. At last, as the hours dragged on, they fell asleep, each profoundly unhappy.

Long ago the two friends had dropped the formality which usually exists between guest and hostess, no matter how intimate. Their relations were as those of two sisters. For the Motor Maids had become as one family in their wanderings together. But next morning, Nancy, still feeling the sting of fancied wrongs, suddenly recalled the fact that she was accepting hospitality from one who no longer liked her. It was all very absurd, but so does the young person at the awkward age between girlhood and womanhood often exaggerate trivial things and enlarge on fancied injustice.

Foolish, pretty Nancy permitted herself to slip into the most extreme state of wretchedness. She imagined that her friend, whom in her heart she loved devotedly, had treated her with unnecessary cruelty and sternness. She got it into her silly little head that Billie had confided the meeting in the garden to the others. She was ashamed and mortified and she felt indeed that the whole world had turned against her. Mr. Campbell was cold to her. Miss Helen Campbell hardly civil Mary and Elinor looked at her askance. There was not a word of truth in it, of course; it was just a figment of Nancy's morbid imaginings. Miss Campbell was bored to extinction with the continued rain. Mr. Campbell was preoccupied because of business engagements of great importance, and Mary and Elinor, if the truth must be told, were intensely homesick; and who would not have been with home on the other side of the world and rain pouring ceaselessly on this side? As for Billie, she tried to be exactly the same as usual, but the cloud of an unsettled disagreement hovered between them.

Therefore after a week of steady rain and black depression which did not seem more profound in Nancy than in anyone else, silly little Nancy took a bold step. Putting on her overshoes and mackintosh late one afternoon, she slipped out of the house and hastened down the avenue. On the road, she hailed an empty 'riksha returning from some suburban home and gave Mme. Fontaine's address in Tokyo.

Nancy was in search of sympathy and of someone who would tell her she had done right when she knew she had done wrong.

Mme. Fontaine was in and would be delighted to see Miss Brown, so she was informed at the widow's front door, and Nancy, a little frightened, now that the deed was done, was ushered into the beautiful drawing-room.

"Why, you sweet child, this is a great pleasure," exclaimed that lady herself, entering at the same moment by another door. "Where are your friends? Are you alone?" she added looking around for the others.

"Oh, yes," answered Nancy, embarrassed and agitated.

"Not even the austere old lady who chaperones you?" asked the other drawing the young girl down beside her on the couch and looking into the blue eyes which suddenly welled up with tears and overflowed,

"Why, my dear, are you unhappy? What is the matter? Tell me all about it," ejaculated Mme. Fontaine, unpinning Nancy's hat and drawing the curly head down on her shoulder.

So it happened that Nancy Brown unburdened herself to the sympathetic Widow of Shanghai, and gave an entirely biased and favorable-to-herself account of the incident in the garden.

Mme. Fontaine sat silent for a while after the story was finished, and Nancy wondered if the charming new friend had heard what she had been saying.

"Do you think Miss Campbell would consent to let you make a visit, Nancy?" she asked presently, calling her Nainsi, as if it were a French name.

Nancy drooped her long lashes.

"I don't know," she answered.

Mme. Fontaine gave one of her inscrutable Mona Lisa smiles and rose from the couch.

"We will try her and see. Does she know you were out walking?"

"No," answered Nancy struggling to keep back her tears.

"Does anyone in the house know?"

She shook her head.

The widow sat down at a carved desk inlaid with mother-of-pearl, and wrote the following note:

"My dear Miss Campbell:

"I trust you will not think I have been unpardonably presumptuous in keeping one of your girls over night with me. She had evidently set out for a long walk and chance brought us together. The child was wet and tired and I have kept her for tea. As the rain is still pouring, she has consented to remain over night with your permission which I cannot but feel sure will be granted under the circumstances. With the very kindest regards for you and your household, I am,

"Faithfully yours,

"ANIELA FONTAINE."

Never was cordial and polite note couched in more non-committal language. It was sent out by a messenger and Miss Campbell sat painfully up in bed to read it. Both knees and one wrist were swathed in bandages of wintergreen liniment and a hot water bottle lay against one hip,

"Why, I didn't know the child had left the house," she exclaimed, when she had finished reading the letter and passed it on to the three remaining Motor Maids. "How did she happen to go alone on a tramp like that? What am I to do? I can't order her to return without being exceedingly rude, but I do wish Nancy hadn't been so reckless. She ought never to have left the grounds alone. Surely the garden is quite large enough for exercising in, if anyone wanted to make the effort."

The little spinster groaned and slipped down among her pillows again.

The girls were silent. Mary secretly sympathized with Nancy. It would be rather fascinating to spend a night in the widow's interesting home. Elinor disapproved slightly at this unconventional visit, but it is doubtful if she would have declined the invitation if she had been in Nancy's place. As for

Billie, she was puzzled and unhappy. She felt sure that there was something back of the departure of her friend. She wished with all her heart they had made up their differences. She yearned for Nancy and her soul was filled with forebodings. She felt somehow as if Nancy had died. That night, with the sheet over her head, she indulged in a fit of weeping and resolved to settle all differences the first moment they could get alone.

Why should Nancy Brown have unexpectedly grown up like this and become so independent and secretive? Elinor, the eldest of the four girls, had never shown a disposition to have affairs and write notes. For her part, Billie would have liked to go on in the same jolly old way forever, with or without beaux. It was all one to her. But Nancy was different. The society of her friends was no longer an unmixed pleasure and she was beginning to crave more excitement and admiration than was good for her.

The next day was like a dozen of its fellows, wet and muggy. The roads were too slippery for the "Comet," and as Miss Campbell still kept her bed with rheumatism, it was decided that Billie should go alone for Nancy in a 'riksha.

She was so eager to make up with her friend, that she felt as if the reconciliation had already taken place and her faithful heart was filled with happiness. She had made up her mind to humble herself by offering Nancy an apology. After all, was it the act of true friendship to pick out all the defects and flaws in a friend's nature?

"A real friend is blind to everything but the best in another friend," reasoned Billie, as her 'riksha splashed along the road, drawn by Komatsu.

So, prepared to embrace Nancy tenderly and let bygones be bygones, Billie could scarcely wait to leap down from the 'riksha and ring the widow's bell. The house had a shut-up appearance, but all Japanese houses look thus in rainy weather.

Somehow, Billie's inflated enthusiasm received a prick when the bell echoed through the rooms with a hollow, empty sound.

She waited impatiently but no one came to answer it. Usually Mme. Fontaine's well-trained maid was bowing and smiling almost before the vibrations of the bell had ceased. Billie rang again and again, and still there was no answer. She walked around the side of the house and peered through the slats of the Venetian blinds but all was dark within.

What could it mean? Where was Nancy? Where was Mme. Fontaine?

"Oh, dear; oh, dear," ejaculated Billie, wiping away the tears that would trickle down her cheeks.

But of course they had gone shopping, and the maid was at market, perhaps. That was the only explanation.

There was a bench on the piazza and Billie sat down to wait. Komatsu stood patiently under his oiled paper umbrella which he always placed in the bottom of the 'riksha in bad weather.

Exactly one hour they waited and at last Billie, disconsolate and disappointed, returned to the 'riksha and ordered Komatsu to take her to some of the shops. Everywhere she watched for the familiar gleam of Nancy's blue mackintosh, but there was no sign of it anywhere. Finally they returned to Mme. Fontaine's house, to find it still closed.

"Komatsu, where are they?" asked Billie desperately.

"Not know, but honorable young lady not look inside?"

"I can't get inside. The doors are locked. Besides, I don't like to break in on a private house like a burglar."

But to the Japanese the end justifies the means, and being on a search for Nancy, Komatsu was willing to go to any strategic lengths to find her.

"All same look and see," he said and together they followed the gallery around the entire house.

"Komatsu make to go up," he said after a fruitless search for an entrance. He pointed to one of the slender pillars which upheld the roof of the lower gallery forming the floor of the upper one. The next moment he had shinned up the pole and Billie could hear him walking softly on the wooden floor above. Presently he returned and placed in Billie's lap the fragments of a letter which had been pieced together and pasted on a sheet of paper.

"Top muchly more easy than bottom," he said smiling. "Empty house but all same muchly inside."

Billie glanced hastily at the scraps of paper and saw her own name in one corner.

"Why, it's to me," she exclaimed, and sitting on the bench, she began to decipher the pieced letter.

"Dear Billie:

"Since you all hate and disapprove of me, I do not wish to stay with you any longer. You have been anything but a friend to me, but I will not say anything more about that. I will only say that I can never forgive what you said to me the other day. I think I have outgrown you. You are just a child still and it will be a long time before you understand the ways of the world, or sympathize with me when I say that I want to broaden my life. Now, Mme. Fontaine, who knows everything, has promised -"

Here the letter broke off.

On the other side of the sheet were some more fragments of

paper carefully pieced together.

> "- do not wish to stay because - father's work - he should not - Mme. - Fontaine thinks -"

Billie folded the paper and slipped it into her pocket. Tears were rolling down her cheeks and she felt suddenly stiff and tired. Komatsu regarded her from a distance with respectful sympathy.

"Back home," she ordered, and all the way she indulged in the bitterest weeping she had ever known in her life.

"Nancy, Nancy, how could you?" she kept repeating to herself.

Before she reached the house she dried her eyes and leaning out of the 'riksha let the rain beat against her face.

"I must think of something to tell them," she said to herself. "What did she mean about Papa's work?"

Again Billie read the last part of the note.

"I believe it's that woman who made her do this," she cried out suddenly. "She worked her up to the point - 'broaden her life' - 'papa's work,' and all that. How could Nancy have thought of such things? And then after Nancy wrote the letter she repented - or perhaps the widow wouldn't let her send it - but how did it happen to be pieced together like this?"

It was all very puzzling and strange. Billie wanted time to think about it and work it out in her own mind, and she was sorry when at last Komatsu came to a full stop at their own front door. Slowly she descended and walked into the house. Suddenly there was a cry of joy from the back. It was the other girls rushing to meet Nancy who had not come, Billie thought miserably.

And, lo, it was Nancy herself, laughing and crying at once and embracing her beloved Billie, as if they had been separated for a year and a day.

"Where did you come from?" Billie managed to gasp in a bewildered voice.

"I got back a little while ago and oh, I've been so homesick. Are you glad to see me, Billie, dearest?"

"I should think I was," said Billie, kissing Nancy's soft round cheek. "It seems an age instead of just one night."

"Mme. Fontaine invited me to make her a visit," went on Nancy, "but - but I was too lonesome - I never slept a wink last night."

"We are all of us quite jealous of you, Nancy," put in Mary, who, with Elinor, had come upon the scene a moment before.

Billie put her hand in her pocket and felt the pieced-together letter. It almost seemed like a bad dream now.

"So you decided to come back to us, Nancy?" she asked, trying to smile naturally.

"If I almost passed away from homesickness in one night, how should I have borne it for - for longer?" answered Nancy, flushing.

"We missed you terribly," was all Billie could trust herself to say as she hurried to her room to take off her wet things.

Just then Onoye sounded the Japanese chimes to announce that luncheon was served and presently they were all assembled around the table.

But never a word did Nancy say about the torn letter which some one had so carefully pieced together.

CHAPTER XV.

THE ANCIENT CITY OF SLEEP.

"How would four young parties and another younger party, who claims to be old and rheumatic, but isn't, like to take a trip?" asked Mr. Campbell one evening at dinner.

Through the inky curtain of blackness that had for days overcast the skies the sun had at last burst with a radiance that seemed twice as great to unaccustomed eyes. From somewhere a life-giving breeze had sprung up and driven away the vapors. Back rolled the walls of mist and fog, and in a few hours the world became a smiling paradise of flowers and of grass and foliage of intensest green.

Immediately the aspect of life changed. Four young parties and a party who claimed to be old but wasn't were eager for anything that would furnish variety after the late monotony of existence.

"I feel," said Mr. Campbell, "that we have all been suffering from certain states of mind that about match the 'Comet's' disguise, and it occurred to me that a change of air would be beneficial."

"And will the 'Cornet' go, too?" asked Billie.

"I'm afraid the 'Comet' is not built for mountain roads in Japan, little daughter," answered her father. "We'll go by train and then by jinrikshas, much as I regret to leave your gasoline pet behind."

"But where are we going?" asked Miss Campbell, in a tone of noble resignation, so chastened were her high spirits by the pains of rheumatism.

"I am going to take you to Nikko to spend a few days, and in order to liven up things a bit the boys are coming, too, even old Mr. Buxton."

"Is -" began Nancy, and checked herself.

"Well, Miss Nancy, 'is' what?" asked Mr. Campbell, smiling.

Billie knew perfectly well that Nancy was going to say: "Is Yoritomo going?" but had changed her mind, when she asked instead:

"Is Nikko a town?"

"It's a number of things. It's considered by some people to be the most beautiful place in the world, for one thing. It's a small town; it's a magnificent forest of cryptomerias; and it's a sacred mountain, and a collection of marvelous old temples and tombs and statues of Buddha. But first and foremost it is a cool, green, lovely spot with good, dry, pine-scented air for certain persons feeling in need of such."

If Mr. Campbell had a fault it was that when he decided to do a thing he wanted to do it at once. Having been a man of camps and considerable lonely wanderings about the world, he had been able to gratify this tendency to decide and act quickly. But it was not so simple with a party of women, and when he announced that they were to start next morning early there was some silent consternation among them.

However, such was the force of Mr. Campbell's personality when he announced a decision that not even that fearless and redoubtable woman, Helen Campbell, had the courage to raise any objections. It was true she had engaged a masseuse at eleven o'clock; the laundry had not been finished; certain persons had planned to shampoo heads, and Mme. Fontaine had asked permission to call in the afternoon.

"All of which things must be postponed and overlooked," thought Miss Campbell.

Mr. Campbell had hired a villa for their short stay. Komatsu was to go along as cook and to carry excess luggage. And they were to take a train at the unearthly hour of eight o'clock a.m., which meant rising at an even more unearthly hour; all of which to a great engineer was a mere trifle.

But who could be in a bad humor on such a glorious morning? Moreover, several funny things happened which set them all laughing as they started off. Komatsu appeared, strung with cooking utensils like a tin man.

"Not muchly good in a renting-house. Komatsu take honorable saucepan," he explained.

In his arms, beside the luncheon hamper, he bore also a beautiful bunch of lilies.

As they climbed into their 'rikshas they were aware of the sound of clipping, and glancing toward the summer-house, beheld twelve old women cutting the grass with large shears. Most of them were widows, as could readily be seen by their short hair. Their worn old faces were wreathed in smiles, when they presently touched their foreheads to the grass in profound obeisances.

"The dear old things," cried Miss Campbell. "O'Haru, do see that they have a good lunch."

No need to give such a command to O'Haru. Refreshments are always given to persons who come in for a day's work in a private place in Japan.

The next amusing incident was the appearance of the old

gardener, Saiki, who came running around the house grasping a bunch of roses.

Giving Mr. Campbell the largest and most beautiful, he divided the others among the ladies.

"Honorable flower for looking on train," he said, with his inimitable smile.

And so, at last they started. All the servants lined up to bid them arespectful farewell. Billie, turning around, saw them gathered in a group on the piazza, fading into spots of bright color in the distance, with the old grass-cutters' robes making a splash of sky blue on the lawn.

"Oh, Nancy," she exclaimed, "there never were such people as the Japanese, so simple and adorable."

Nancy, engaged in pinning a rose on the lapel of her coat and looking at the effect with her pocket mirror, made no reply.

At the railroad station they were met by Reggie, Nicholas and Mr. Buxton. Everybody was in the wildest spirits because of the change in the weather, and as they crowded, laughing and jostling each other, into the train, the Japanese travelers smiled good-naturedly. They liked to see Americans enjoying the country.

Scarcely had they settled themselves in the train when they became aware that two Japanese women were smiling and bowing repeatedly in the most cordial manner.

"Why, it's Mme. Ito," exclaimed Miss Campbell.

"And O'Kami San," finished Mary, who remembered names for everybody.

"Are you going to Nikko, too, O'Kami San?" asked Billie, sitting beside the pretty little Japanese.

O'Kami San looked much embarrassed and hung her head.

"Make honorable journey to husband's home," she said in a low voice.

"Have you been getting married?" demanded Billie, astonished.

"Yesterdays passing four," answered O'Kami San.

"You mean four days ago?"

"Yes, honorable Mees Cam-el."

Both Japanese women were beautifully dressed and it came out during the conversation that the young bride was wearing no less than five elaborate kimonos.

"But why?" demanded Billie.

O'Kami San explained that it was to avoid the inconveniences of luggage. They were going to a little town in the hills and it would be difficult to carry trunks.

Around her head the bride wore a broad band of pink silk, almost covering her hair, to keep the horns of jealousy from growing.

Billie looked at her pityingly.

"Poor little thing," she thought. "Why doesn't that good-for-nothing brother teach her something? It doesn't seem to me that his schooling did him any good. He's so fanatical and bigoted."

"I hope you will be very happy, O'Kami San," said Mary. "I believe you said there was no mother-in-law."

"Not no mother-in-law," answered the bride, in the tone of

one describing a great blessing. "Honorable husband of age like mother-in-law."

"You mean your husband is not young?"

O'Kami San nodded.

"Verily old," she said, with just the faintest quiver at the corners of her mouth.

Mary and Billie regarded her with compassion. How little romance there was in a Japanese girl's life! O'Kami San, so young and pretty and charming, too, was about to enter into years of drudgery perhaps; the wife of a cranky old man, and here she was accepting her fate as calmly as a novitiate about to take the vows for life and enter a convent.

"New husband much rich," she said. "Much old. Need attentionly young wife."

Only once did O'Kami San glance at the two handsome young men who belonged to the Campbell party. But Nicholas, always gallant and thoughtful, helped Mme. Ito and her daughter to alight at the way-station where they were to change cars, while Reggie carried their small belongings and placed them on the platform.

"God bless you, O'Kami San," called Billie, leaning far out of the window. And if the little Japanese girl did not understand the meaning of the salutation she comprehended the spirit of it.

"Receive thanks," she said formally, her eyes glistening suspiciously. Then she gave the Japanese farewell, "Sayonara" (since it must be), and waved her little hands until the train was out of sight.

Billie watched her sadly. The lines of the five kimonos, which could be distinctly counted where they crossed at her neck, seemed to symbolize the heavy marriage yoke the little bride had slipped so uncomplainingly over her head, and as for that pink silk head band to keep down the horns of jealousy, it might just as well have been an iron band with spikes in it, for all the sentiment and romance it represented. But little O'Kami San had gone up into the hills to her aged husband, and if she guessed that there was anything brighter and happier than just being an "attentionly wife" to an old man, she never murmured. No one has ever plumbed the depths of unselfishness and self-sacrifice of the little Japanese wife.

During the last few miles of the journey they left the train and took to jinrikshas. Along a magnificent avenue they rode, built through a forest of cryptomerias towering one hundred and eighty feet high, some of them with trunks thirty feet in diameter. They were like the columns of a gigantic cathedral of which the sky was the dome.

After refreshing themselves with tea at their little villa and removing the grime of the journey, the travelers wandered off into the ancient forest, cool and gray and very still, except for the sound of the wind whispering through the pine trees.

Terraced stairways of gray stone climb up the mountainside from temple to temple and court to court. Over a busy little river hung the scarlet bridge of beauty which no profane foot may ever touch, only the Emperor's consecrated feet. No human hand has mended the sacred bridge for nearly three centuries, but it is said to be in perfect repair.

Passing along the temples and shrines that crowded one another on the hillside, they came at last to a row of images of Buddha, innumerable stone statues of the god, his kindly, gentle face almost obliterated by spray from the river and a soft mantle of moss. There is a tradition which says that no two people have ever counted these images with the same results, and while the others wandered up the next terraced flight of steps, Billie and Mary remained to count the Buddhas.

The loud song of the little river rushing by them dazed their senses and when they reached the end Billie had counted eighty and Mary only seventy-five.

"Let's try again," said Billie; once more they followed the interminable line and once more there was a wide discrepancy between the results.

For the third time they started the count, and finally came as near as seventy-eight and seventy-nine; but the act of counting and recounting had a curious effect on their senses. It seemed to make them very sleepy, or perhaps it was the magic of that ancient place, the monotonous song of the torrent and the cool gray shadows in the depths of the forest where the sun never penetrated.

"Do you know, Billie, I think I'll have to rest a moment before we join the others," said Mary, leading the way up the hillside and sitting down under a giant pine tree. "I'm almost paralyzed with sleep."

"I feel the same way," answered Billie drowsily. "We can catch up with them later. Suppose we take a little repose, as a French lady I knew used to say."

The two girls removed their hats, and making pillows of their jackets they stretched themselves on the soft carpet of pine needles. Presently, lulled by the monotonous water song and the murmur of the wind through the trees, they dropped off into a sleep so profound and deep that they did not hear the voices of their friends returning to search for them.

The enchantment of centuries had woven its net about their feet and stilled their senses; for Nikko is called the "City of Rest," and an endless number of saints and holy men who once lived and prayed among its groves now sleep there.

The two young girls sank deeper and deeper into the peaceful sleep which the atmosphere of Nikko breathes. Their souls seemed to have entered the region of the most profound rest that may come to a living person.

And while they slept the sun sank and the twilight of the forest faded into night. But the searchers had taken the wrong path and their cries grew fainter and fainter as they ranged the mountainside for the lost girls. Among the trees their paper lanterns glowed like fireflies and occasionally there was a long cry: "A-hai!"

But Buddha himself must have placed the seal of sleep on the young girls' eyes.

CHAPTER XVI.

THE STORM KING.

While two of the Motor Maids slept in the sacred wood on the mountain two others rested in one of the bedrooms of the villa straining their ears for sounds of the returning search party. It was only eight o'clock, but Miss Campbell, worn out with excitement and fatigue, had already dropped off to sleep in the next room.

Nancy was quietly and softly weeping, her face buried in her pillow, and Elinor lay staring into the darkness. Mr. Campbell had assured them that the girls could not be lost for long, and that the only mishap that could possibly come to them in that holy place was sleeping under the pine trees; but he could not conceal the anxiety he really felt, the anxiety of a father for his only daughter, the being he loved best in all the world.

Nancy had felt the anxiety, too, and remorse had entered into her soul; not because she had met Yoritomo in the garden and exchanged notes with him in a romantic manner, the notes having been hidden under a stone near the old shrine, for she was beginning dimly to realize that such things were only silly and common. Her remorse was caused by something else more remote in her consciousness but looming bigger all the time. The cruel letter she had written to Billie in anger and then torn into pieces and thrown into a brass vase in Mme. Fontaine's drawing-room! Why had she been so angry? She could not understand it now. She only knew that the longer she poured her troubles into Mme. Fontaine's ears the more sympathetic the widow became until Nancy was worked into a perfect rage.

As for the widow, she had said very little indeed, only a few words now and then, vague, suggestive remarks, but they had set Nancy thinking; had stirred her up so violently, indeed, that she had written that foolish letter. There had been no waste basket by the desk and Nancy, after a wretched sleepless night, had torn up the letter and dropped it in the nearest vase. Why had she not torn it into smaller bits? Why had she not burned it in a charcoal brazier? Why had she ever written it at all? Why - why - ? A dozen whys flashed through her troubled mind. She would never rest again until she knew the letter had been entirely destroyed, reduced to ashes. Out of this long train of unhappy thought a resolution came to Nancy to write to Mme. Fontame and ask her to find the letter and burn it up. This she accordingly did a few days after the visit to Nikko, and of what came of it more will be told later.

In the meantime, while Nancy, goaded by a troubled conscience was weeping abundantly into her pillow, Billie and little Mary Price lay sleeping peacefully in the great cathedral forest.

Precisely at the moment that Nancy's disturbed fancies had taken the form of a resolution Billie and Mary opened their eyes on a world of velvety blackness. Straight overhead through the lacework of intertwined boughs gleamed an occasional tiny star, like the light shining through a pin prick in a black curtain. Scarcely two hours had passed since they had slipped into the unknown, and now sitting up and rubbing their eyes, they wondered where in the world they were. Hearing Mary stirring beside her in the dark, Billie put out a hand and grasped Mary's groping to meet it. The two friends sat silently for a few minutes. At last Billie said softly:

"What are we going to do, Mary, dear?"

"I am thinking of what they are going to do," answered Mary. "How frightened they will be about us, Billie! As for me, I can't help feeling happy out in this dark peaceful place. I should like to lie here all night and watch the dawn come through the trees."

All of which was extremely poetic, but Billie had become suddenly prosaic at the thought of her father, wild with anxiety she was certain, searching the terraced mountainside for them at the risk of falling off a precipice or tumbling into the river. Besides, at that moment, she felt a puff of hot wind in her face, and immediately was conscious that she was very thirsty and that the palms of her hands were dry and burning.

"Don't you think it's very hot, Mary?" she whispered. "I feel as if I had been baked brown in an oven."

"The wind has changed," answered Mary. "It was cool and sweet when we dropped off, and now it's like a wind that's blown over a desert."

Through the forest came a murmur like thousands of voices gathering in strength and volume all the time. The gigantic pillars of the cathedral began swaying and tossing their arched boughs and the whole mountain seemed to resound with strange sounds, cries and calls, grindings and poundings. The pin prick stars disappeared and the place was as black as the pit.

The two girls rose quickly and clasped hands again.

"I think we'd better go straight down," said Billie. "We're obliged to strike a path somewhere and perhaps we may find a temple or a tomb or a pagoda or something. Anything to get away from that awful thing that's coming, whatever it is."

Fortunately the act of descending gave them a sense of direction. Many times they fell, skinning their shins and their foreheads against trees, but they picked themselves up again, entirely unconscious of bruises, and ran on as fast as they could go with the hot devastating wind behind them. Suddenly the whole mountainside was illuminated by a flash of lightning, like a jagged stream of fire stretching from heaven to earth. A deafening roar of thunder followed. Then all the forest seemed to be perfectly quiet. Such a stillness settled over the place that the girls stopped and held their breath.

"Look," whispered Billie, pointing to a strange looking light coming rapidly nearer, wobbling and undulating like the light on the bow of a ship in a rough ocean. Then came another terrifying flash of lightning, and thunder that seemed to rock the whole world. The two girls rushed toward the friendly light with one accord, and collided with the bearer with such force that three persons were precipitated with unintentionally devotional attitudes at the foot of a shrine of Buddha.

"By Jove, but this is luck," called a familiar voice.

It was Nicholas Grimm, who calmly picked up himself and then his oil-paper lantern attached to the end of a slender wand; next he helped the girls to their feet.

"Take an arm, each one of you. There's no time to lose. The thing that's coming, whatever it is, will get here in a minute now."

Running like mad, on the very wings of the wind, the three young people followed the windings of the path and presently came up short on a small temple, the tomb of some holy personage. Into this they rushed without ceremony just as the storm burst with all its fury, and crouching in a corner just out of reach of the rain, they listened to the howls and shrieks of the wind.

"It's just like some live thing," remarked Mary after a while. "I feel as if some terrible demon lived up in a cave in the mountain, and when he is angry he comes down and lashes the earth and shakes the mountain."

Mary's poetic notion of storms in that region was not so far removed from the Japanese legends.

"You struck the nail on the head that time, Miss Price," said Nicholas.

"There is an extinct volcano over here in the northeast and in its side is a huge cavern. People around here used to believe that all these frightful storms issued from the cavern. Every spring and every fall there was a perfectly corking one that tore up the whole place, and they called the mountain 'Ni-Ko San,' or Two-Storm Mountain. Then an old party who was a saint, I believe, and very wise, placed a curse on the storm demon and named the place 'Nikko San,' Mountain of the Sun's Brightness."

"The demon seems to have returned," remarked Billie.

"Oh, he did. That was the point. The magic curse had to be repeated every year, and the saint gave the receipt to a priest and it was handed down from one generation to another in the priest's family for nearly nine hundred years, but the demon still pursued, as you have probably observed."

They were all silent for a while. Mary was making a picture in her mind of the aged priest in his white robes standing like a midget on the side of the vast mountain exorcising the storm king. That personage, she imagined, was a gigantic figure formed principally of black clouds with a terrifying human countenance. Every breath was a whirlwind or a hailstorm and when he struck the side of the mountain with his staff the lightning flashed -

Here Mary's thoughts were interrupted by just such a flash uncomfortably near.

Billie leaped to her feet.

"Oh, Nicholas," she cried, "do you think Papa could still be looking for me? Suppose he should be out now in all this frightful wind! I hadn't thought of it until this moment."

"He'll be all right, Miss Billie," answered Nicholas soothingly. "Don't you worry."

"Don't you tell me not to worry," cried Billie, almost angrily. "Do you think Papa would look after himself if he thought I was lost on the mountain? Oh, heavens, why did we count those old broken statues?"

Nicholas laughed.

"Excuse me," he said, choking back his amusement at sight of Billie's reproachful eyes which even the dim lantern light could not hide. "What are you going to do?" he added, as Billie seized the lantern from his hand.

"I'm going to wave this at the door and yell with all my strength until I haven't any voice left. If Papa is anywhere near he may see it and come straight here."

Nicholas, who, having also had much training in camps and outdoor life, had not felt the least uneasiness about Mr. Campbell's safety, now quietly took the lantern from Billie and began waving it to and fro at the door, while they both shouted again and again. But their voices were lost in the roar of the tempest. Billie stifled a sob.

"Papa!" she whispered to herself. "Dearest, dearest Papa!"

While she spoke a flash of lightning lit up the side of the mountain, and in that momentary illumination Billie saw her father toiling up the path against the wind and rain.

"Papa, Papa!" she shrieked, seizing the lantern and waving it wildly back and forth.

"Halloo!" yelled Nicholas, and then there came an answering shout, a really human cry this time, and after several breathless moments of waiting Mr. Campbell staggered into the temple.

Nicholas and Mary turned their faces away at sight of his emotion when he found his daughter in his arms. He actually buried his face on her shoulder and wept like a child.

"I was beginning to think I was never going to see you again, sweetheart," he said brokenly.

It gave Mary a lonesome, remote feeling. She drew away from the others into a corner of the temple and rested her chin on her hands.

"I wonder how it would feel to have some one big and strong and - and handsome to love and protect one like that," she thought contemplatively.

Just then a figure staggered into the circle of light cast by the lantern. It was Mr. Buxton.

"Good evening," he said. "Delightful weather, isn't it? Suppose we shed a little light on Carlton's path," he added calmly, holding the light to the door. Reggie was close behind his friend, however, and with feelings of enormous relief, the little company proceeded to sit down on the floor and relate their experiences.

"It all really happened," remarked Mary, after Billie had confessed the cause of all the trouble, "because we tried to count the four hundred statues of Buddha and never got the same answer twice, and he naturally didn't like it, and I suppose he put us to sleep and summoned the Storm King -"

"No, child," interrupted Mr. Buxton, "I am sorry to disabuse your romantic young mind, but it really happened because the pressure of the coming storm had a stupefying effect. Buddha was a very high-minded gentleman. He would never have taken offence over such a trivial matter."

"Don't contradict her, Buxton," said Mr. Campbell. "You have no imagination to comprehend the supernatural, anyhow."

"It would be supernatural for two women to count alike,"

answered the incorrigible bachelor, who would have the last word.

Gradually the storm spent its fury, and by midnight they were able to return to the little villa. Except for a few scratches and bruises, the only important result of the Storm King's visit was Nancy's determination to write a letter to Mme. Fontaine.

CHAPTER XVII.

A VISIT OF CEREMONY.

The most unhappy person in the whole of fair Japan was Miss Nancy Brown one lovely morning in July. At least she thought she was; which is very near to being the same thing. She had dispatched a letter to Mme. Fontaine and received an answer that the brass vase by the writing desk was now empty - a curious way to put it, Nancy thought, and one which did not quiet her uneasiness in the least. In return for this bit of information the Widow of Shanghai asked a strange favor of Nancy, one which puzzled and troubled her considerably. But it was a simple request and Nancy could not see any reason for declining to grant it.

So, Mistress Nancy was the prey to indefinable anxieties and vague forebodings. Everybody had noticed her sadness. Mr. Campbell had spoken of it with concern and had promised to take them all on another trip to the mountains.

"The heat is too much for the child," he had remarked to his cousin. "I didn't realize she was such a fragile little thing. Even Mary Price seems more robust."

"She never was a fragile little thing before, Duncan," answered Miss Campbell. "I always thought that Billie and Nancy had unlimited endurance. The other girls are much more delicate. Do you suppose Nancy has anything on her mind?"

Mr. Campbell shook his head. It was impossible for him to think that any of those light-hearted creatures could have troubles. They had nothing to think about but their own pleasures; nothing to do but enjoy the house and the garden, the tea parties and excursions. Their happy laughter and gay chatter, floating to him through the open window of his library did not carry a single note of sadness; for Nancy had tried to cover her unhappiness under a cloak of forced gaiety; but she could not hide her tragic little face, nor the pathetic droop of her lips and the circles under her eyes.

"I can never look Billie in the face again," she had said to herself a hundred times. "I almost feel as if I had murdered somebody and hidden the body away. Nobody knows about the letter but it's just as bad as if they did. I believe I couldn't be more miserable if I had sent it to Billie. Thinking is just as bad as saying things out loud, and writing them seems to make it even worse."

Furthermore, Onoye had been acting very strangely toward Nancy lately. Twice she had come and stood before the American girl with downcast eyes and twice tried to say something, failed and slipped quietly away.

On this wonderful Sunday morning, when the world seemed indescribably fresh and fair after the recent rains, only Nancy was sad. Mary, who had blossomed into a flower herself in the soft warm air of Japan, was fairly dancing along the walk.

"There is so much to do," she cried. "I haven't a moment to spare. The red lilies are in bloom. They all live together in a place near the old shrine. Saiki says if the weather keeps on like this the lotus flowers in the pond will open. Over against the old south wall there is a climbing rose bush that is a perfect marvel. You see, Saiki tells me all the secrets of the garden. He and I are the most devoted friends."

The girls smiled indulgently at Mary, who seemed to them to have developed in a few weeks from a timid, shrinking little soul with a tinge of sadness in her nature into the most joyous being.

"Go on and tell us some more," put in Elinor. "I like to hear all this garden gossip. You'll be hearing the secret the white rose whispered to the red next; and how the sensitive plant shrank when she heard the news, and the lilies shut up -"

"And the flags waved and the grasses drew their blades, and the trees barked and the cow slips and the bull rushes -" cried Billie. And they all burst into absurd laughter, that is, all except Nancy, who felt immensely remote from this foolish, pleasant talk.

"It will never do for you to be a teacher, Mary, dearest," said Elinor. "You'd simply fade and droop in a schoolroom. We'll just have to look up some other occupation for you. If I had my way with Providence you should do nothing but play in a garden all your days in a land of perpetual summer."

"I am afraid I should have to pass into another world to accomplish anything so wonderful," laughed Mary. "It sounds a good deal like Paradise to me, and I haven't learned to play my harp yet. I would never be admitted into such a beautiful garden until I had learned to play real music on the harp, and not discords."

Mary often spoke in metaphors like this, which half puzzled, half amused her friends.

"I never heard you strike a discord, Mary, dear," Nancy observed sadly, when Billie interrupted:

"Canst tell me who that grand personage is riding up the avenue?"

In a jinriksha drawn by one man, while two others ran in front to clear the way of imaginary obstacles, since there were no real ones, sat a magnificent person clad in full Japanese regalia. He wore a robe of dark rich colors, but the girls could not see his face, which was hidden by a parasol.

"I think Nankipooh has come to call," whispered Billie, as the vehicle drew near.

The girls hid themselves behind a clump of shrubbery and peeped through the branches.

"He's bringing gifts," whispered Elinor.

The 'riksha had drawn up at the piazza and the two runners, after the personage in fancy dress had descended, lifted out a very aged and no doubt extremely costly dwarfed apple tree growing in a green vase, and a lacquered box.

One of the ever-watchful domestics opened the door and into the hall stalked the visitor, followed by his retainers.

"I think he must be a messenger from the Emperor, nothing less," said Billie. "He's so awfully grand."

"Perhaps he's the Mikado himself," said Mary.

The others laughed again and even Nancy forgot her troubles and joined in.

"I declare I feel as if I had settled down to live on a Japanese fan," continued Billie. "Everything is like a decoration. I can't imagine anything really serious ever happening, it's all so gay and pretty and the people are like dolls."

"Here comes one of your live dolls," observed Mary, pointing to Onoye, who was hastening toward them down the path, the skirts of her flowered kimono blowing about her ankles as she walked.

She made straight for the group of girls and falling on her knees before Nancy, touched her forehead to the ground.

"What is it, Onoye?" asked Nancy, blushing and paling and blushing again with some hidden emotion.

KATHERINE STOKES

"Gracious lady, warn-ings," she began slowly, as if she had just learned the words from a book.

"What on earth?" Nancy asked.

"Gracious lady, warn-ings," repeated Onoye, in a monotonous voice.

"What do you mean, Onoye?" demanded Billie. "Don't kneel. Stand up and tell us all about it."

"No explaining words to make understanding. Make prayer to honorable Mees Nancee."

"But what about?" asked Nancy, puzzled and troubled at the same time.

"Dee-vorce," answered Onoye, and then touching her forehead to the ground, she rose quickly and glided away.

It was so absurd that they were obliged to laugh, and yet they felt that the Japanese girl was entirely serious in what she was trying to tell.

"Can't we call her back and ask her some more questions?" suggested Elinor.

"We might, but I doubt if she would say another word," answered Billie. "They never will tell more than they have to, you know, and I daresay she thinks she's told all that is necessary."

"I think she's got hold of the wrong words," put in Mary. "Do you remember how she called Miss Campbell 'the honorable old maid'?"

"She has had something on her mind a long time," said Billie thoughtfully. "She's a queer little soul. You don't think she could be a bit daffy, do you?"

"I never saw any signs of it," said Nancy. "But I do wish she had explained why I was to be warned. Perhaps she's got that word wrong, too."

"The truth is, the Japanese use synonyms instead of the words themselves. That's why their English is so queer," remarked Mary, better trained in English than any of the others and with a remarkably good vocabulary when she could be persuaded to talk. "Now a synonym of 'to warn' is 'to summon.' Maybe Onoye wanted to tell you that some one wished to see you."

Nancy was silent. She vaguely connected Onoye's visit with Mme. Fontaine and the note, because her thoughts constantly dwelt on those disquieting subjects.

The girls lingered for some time in the garden until they saw the Japanese gentleman in fancy dress riding away in his 'riksha, preceded by his two runners. Once more Onoye approached them down one of the shady garden walks. Once more she paused in front of Nancy and prostrating herself, announced:

"The honorable master in libraree to Mees Brown."

Nancy turned as white as a sheet.

"Why, Nancy, don't be frightened. I am sure it's nothing serious," said Billie, putting her arm around her friend's waist.

Except for that first greeting when Billie had returned after her search for Nancy, it was the first time the two girls had stood thus since the letter episode, and it was too much for poor, contrite Nancy, who burst into tears.

"She thinks it's bad news from home," said Mary, leaning a cheek sympathetically against Nancy's shoulder, while Elinor pressed her hand and exclaimed:

"Dearest, dearest Nancy, I'm sure it's nothing sad. Don't cry."

If anything could have made Nancy more wretched, it was the sympathy of her three friends.

"I don't deserve it, I don't deserve it!" she sobbed, and except for Billie, they had not the remotest idea what she meant.

And now in the midst of this highly emotional scene appeared Miss Helen Campbell accompanied by Messrs. Campbell, Buxton, Carlton and Grimm. There was an arch and knowing smile on Miss Campbell's face as she tripped along the walk holding a lavender parasol over her head, and the four men were grinning broadly. Nancy dried her tears quickly. They never left any traces on her face nor red rims around her eyelids as with most people, and except that she was unusually pale, no one would have guessed that her lachrymal ducts had been overflowing only a moment before.

"Well, well, Miss Nancy, I am afraid we shall have to put smoked glasses over those pretty blue eyes of yours before they cause any more mischief in Japan," exclaimed Mr. Campbell.

"Oh, you little witch," cried Miss Campbell, pinching Nancy's cheek, "what shall I do with you, making eyes at these Orientals who don't understand?"

"But what -" began Nancy.

"I know," cried Mary, the gleam of romance in her eyes, "I know now. She's gone and got proposed to by a Japanese gentleman!"

"But who?" cried all the girls together, brimming over with curiosity.

"Why, Mr. Yoritomo Ito, of course," replied Miss Campbell. "He dressed up in his best Japanese fancy costume and brought presents and servants and came to ask formally for the hand of Mistress Anne Starbuck Brown."

"Why, the impudent thing," exclaimed Nancy. "Did he think - could he imagine for a moment -"

She broke off, too indignant to express herself. Then her eyes encountered Billie's and she dropped them in embarrassment. They were both thinking of the same thing; the two notes left under a stone at the shrine and the rainy meeting in the garden. After all, perhaps Yoritomo might have thought she liked him - but the idea was intolerable and Nancy thrust it aside.

"How would you like to be mother-in-lawed by Mme. Ito, Nancy?" asked Elinor.

"And sleep with your head on a bench and eat with chop sticks?" continued Mary.

"You would probably have to do all those things if you married Mr. Yoritomo Ito," said Mr. Campbell. "It's very evident that he belongs to the most conservative Japanese class and clings to the old notions about wives and fancy dress costumes and such things."

"What did you say to him, Papa?" asked Billie.

"Oh, I was very polite, of course. I declined his offer, but that didn't surprise him, because in Japan they never stop to consult a young lady about her choice. They make it for her and then inform her afterward. Was I right in my method of dismissing your suitor, Miss Nancy?" he asked, turning to the young girl with a certain charming manner that was peculiarly his own, half humorous and half deferential.

"Oh, yes, Mr. Campbell," exclaimed Nancy, a flush spreading over her face. "I am ashamed that it ever happened. I'm sure I never meant him to think - I'm sure I can't understand his presuming -"

"Never mind, child. Men propose the world over without any

more grounds than that. They are all alike, yellow skins and white ones, and red ones, too," said Miss Campbell.

"Don't be so hard on us, Madam," put in Mr. Buxton, seizing the lady's parasol by force and holding it firmly over her head. "It's not our fault if we fall victims to a pair of blue eyes. You notice I say 'victims.' One pair has many, I presume."

Billie and Nicholas brought up the procession which was now moving slowly toward the pavilion.

"It's queer that I just learned something about Yoritomo last night," said Nicholas, "and I was going to tell you to-day."

"What is it?" asked Billie.

"He's divorced. You know they get them here on the slightest provocation - just change their minds after a few months or years and go to court, and one morning a wife finds herself without a husband, or children either, if he wants to take them."

"How perfectly outrageous for him to propose to Nancy!" cried Billie. "You don't know who his first wife was, do you, Nicholas?"

"No, I didn't hear."

"I think I do," said Billie, after a moment's pause.

CHAPTER XVIII.

THE MAGNET AND THE SILVER CHURN.

"Is it your head, dear? Are you sure nothing else is involved? No indigestion or pains at the neck or burning at the pit of the stomach?"

"Perfectly certain, Miss Campbell," answered Nancy, with a wan smile. "It's just one of those sick headaches like the one I had when I ate crab salad and peach ice cream that time. You mustn't stay at home on my account. O'Haru will look after me."

"But you haven't eaten crab salad and peach ice cream this time, child. You haven't eaten anything, in fact. Your appetite is getting smaller all the time."

"It's just the heat," said Nancy meekly. "I only want to stay in a darkened room and keep as cool as I can. I am sure I shall be all right by this evening and I wouldn't for anything interfere with the picnic to-day. It would make my head much worse. Really it would."

Each of the Motor Maids offered to stay home with Nancy, but she objected and protested so strongly that it looked as if she would work herself into a fever if they persisted. O'Haru was therefore left in charge of Nancy for the day, while the others, attired for an all-day picnic, gathered on the front piazza.

On the driveway stood the "Comet" and behind him at a

KATHERINE STOKES

respectful distance, like a servant behind his master, stood another car of an undistinguished character, hired in Tokyo. Into this last climbed Miss Campbell and Mr. Buxton, while Mr. Campbell took the front seat to run the car.

"Won't some little maid keep a lonely man company?" he called, and Mary Price responded promptly to this appeal. "I am the most honored man in the whole party," he said, gallantly jumping out and helping her in as if she were a small queen.

Mary smiled happily, but she felt in her heart that she was the most honored of all. No one had ever treated her with such deference and courtesy as this splendid big man who gazed down at her with a protecting air and listened to her rather timid conversation with absorbed interest.

It was a wonderful thing, Mary thought, almost too wonderful to be believed that a distinguished engineer who had been sent for by governments to build railroads and give advice about public improvements, would condescend even to notice a quiet little person like her. But the famous engineer was really a very simple man, as modest as she herself was and quite as gentle.

On the front seat beside Billie sat Nicholas, and Reginald was in the back with Elinor. Every laddie had a lassie that morning, and Billie, who was a bit skeptical over Nancy's headache, wondered vaguely if this could have been the reason for her staying at home. But she put the thought away from her at once as being unworthy. Billie sighed and gave herself an impatient little shake. Her heart yearned for the old Nancy of the early days who seemed so changed now. She was determined never to mention the letter, but somehow it seemed always to stand between them. Both girls thought of it constantly, Nancy with remorse and bitterness for her own disloyalty, and Billie with a kind of puzzled sadness. After all, the two friends had much to learn about each other's natures.

Nancy on her bed in the darkened room was saying:

"If I only could prove to Billie and to all of them that I am not disloyal!"

Billie, guiding the "Comet" along the country road, was thinking:

"If Nancy would only be frank and tell me what's on her mind! How can we go on like this when we are drifting farther and farther away?"

The excursion to-day was of special interest to Mr. Campbell and his guests. They were riding forth to see Fujiyama (or "Fuji San," as the Japanese call it, "yama," meaning simply "mountain"), the sacred mountain of perfect beauty and shining whiteness.

Once Saiki, their old gardener, had conducted them to a small elevation in the garden, and in a manner both reverential and proud, had pointed to a vista in the trees carefully made by lopping off certain branches. There, in the background of a long, narrow perspective loomed the great mountain, exactly as it does in thousands of Japanese scrolls. Here, many a time, Mary had sat and watched the white cone shining in the sunlight. She understood why it was called the "Peak of the White Lotus," The low green hills at its feet were the leaves of the flower and the eight sided crater, perfect in symmetry, formed the petals.

The beautiful Fuji San, the most precious and revered object in all Japan, is dedicated to a goddess, "the Princess who makes the blossoms of the trees to bear"; but pilgrims of every religious sect crowd its paths in warm weather and on its sides dwell holy men or "mountain worshippers," who practice great austerities.

It seemed a little unfeeling to be so gay and light-hearted with Nancy unhappy and ill at home, but there was gaiety in the warm dry air, and it bubbled into happy laughter and chatter as they flew along the road.

"Have we brought everything?" called Billie over her shoulder. "The guitar and the tea basket and the luncheon hamper -"

"And the mackintoshes?" finished Nicholas.

Billie frowned and her face darkened.

"Everything but your raincoat, Billie," said Elinor, counting packages in the bottom of the car with the toe of her boot. "Did you forget it?"

"No, it had a torn place in it," answered Billie, still frowning.

An incident too trivial to mention, but too unusual to put lightly aside had caused her some annoyance that morning. She had closed the bureau drawer on a corner of her raincoat, hanging over her arm, and had torn the hem off one side.

"How stupid," she had exclaimed impatiently, tossing it into a chair. "You'll have to lend me your blue raincoat, Nancy-Bell. I've just done for mine completely."

Nancy, lying on the bed with her face turned to the wall, did not reply.

Billie tiptoed to the foot of the bed to see if she was asleep, but the blue eyes were wide open staring at the wall paper.

"Will you lend me your raincoat, Miss Nancy?" repeated Billie, trying to be jocular to overcome the peculiar sensation of annoyance that had crept into her thoughts.

"I'm sorry, but I can't," answered Nancy, in a low voice.

"Why not?"

"I just can't. That's all."

Billie felt as if a rough hand had seized her by her collar and given her a good shaking.

"Oh, very well, Nancy" she said, and went softly out of the room.

"I am sure she must be really ill," she thought, trying to put a charitable interpretation on this act of selfishness, but even illness could hardly account for anything so entirely remote from their usual relations. And, apparently, Nancy had no fever and was only a little under the weather with a headache.

Therefore, when the subject of her raincoat had come under discussion, Billie quickly changed it.

"Do look at that queer-looking crowd," she ejaculated, pointing to a group of people walking in couples along the roadside. Their white kirtles were girded high about their waists and they carried staffs.

As the company marched along, always facing Fuji, they began singing a weird chant. When the motors drew nearer the tourists saw that each man wore a huge mushroom hat made of lightest pith and from his neck hung a piece of matting suspended by a cord.

"That must be one of the Pilgrim Clubs," announced Nicholas. "There are hundreds of them in Japan and they are fearfully expensive to join. The dues are from eight to fifteen cents a year. Every summer a club selects a delegate to take a nice little walking trip to a shrine and bring back blessings for the other members. His expenses are paid and lots of the other members go on their own hook. All the inns make special rates and it's come to be a jolly way to spend one's vacation, combining pleasure and religion. You see they've got the costume down to the finest point," he continued. "They wear umbrellas on their heads, and the matting hanging around their necks serves as a raincoat, seat and bed. It's the coolest, lightest and most complete walking equipment I ever saw."

"They make me feel terribly worldly-minded and luxurious," exclaimed Billie. "I never thought of bringing back a holy blessing to a friend."

"We can take back a blessing for Miss Nancy, if you like," said Nicholas, smiling. "A flask of water from a spring on the sacred mountain would do, wouldn't it?"

"But we haven't any flask."

"We have the thermos bottle," put in Elinor. "That would keep it cool enough for her to drink."

"She shouldn't drink it. She should sprinkle herself with it, or bathe in it," said Nicholas, amused at this ultra-modern way of carrying back a heavenly blessing.

But Billie recalled the suggestion later and actually did fill the thermos bottle from a little spring that bubbled at the foot of Fuji and trickled down a green slope where the company had stopped for luncheon.

"I do wish Nancy had come," she found herself saying while she spread the white cloth on the grass and opened the treasures of the luncheon hamper, which consisted of cold chicken and sandwiches and eggs prepared in a peculiar pickly way, as some one had described it. "It was a shame for her to miss this lovely trip. I am sure Fuji would have cured anybody's headache. It's so beautiful and so majestic."

"It's cured mine," remarked Mr. Buxton, "either Fuji or something even more potent." Here he cast a languishing and eloquent glance toward Miss Campbell who flicked the grass with the end of her parasol and pretended not to have heard a word.

Nicholas and Reggie grinned openly. Mr. Campbell stifled a smile behind a large sandwich and the girls carefully avoided each other's eyes.

"He's got it bad, Miss Billie," whispered Nicholas. "Is this a common occurrence with Miss Campbell?"

"It is, indeed," answered Billie. "There is always one and sometimes several wherever we go. Once, in Salt Lake City, it saved us no end of trouble and brought two lovers together, because a horrid old Mormon gentleman caught the fever. He had it so badly that we thought he would just carry Cousin Helen off by force, but he was deathly afraid of her."

"Remember your promise, Miss Elinor," called Mr. Campbell presently. "Where's your guitar?"

Some one fetched the guitar from the car and Elinor, leaning against a tree, struck several chords and smiled mischievously.

"Shall it be a love song?" she asked.

"Something religious would be more appropriate in this sacred spot," observed Miss Campbell severely. But Elinor, ignoring the suggestion, began to sing:

> "'O, My Luve's like a red, red rose,
> That's newly sprung in June.
> My Luve's like the melodie
> That's sweetly played in tune.
>
> "'As fair thou art, my bonnie lass,
> So deep in luve am I,
> And I will luve thee still, my dear,
> Till a' the seas gang dry.
>
> "'Till a' the seas gang dry, my dear,
> And rocks melt wi' the sun,
> I will luve thee still, my dear,
> While the sands of life shall run.
>
> "'And fare thee weel, my only Luve,
> And fare thee weel a while,

And I will come again My Luve,
Tho' it were ten thousand mile.'"

While Elinor sang this charming song Mr. Buxton regarded Miss Helen Campbell with an expression so abjectly adoring that Mr. Campbell gave a roar of boyish laughter and laid himself flat on the ground in the ecstasy of his amusement. They all laughed, indeed. Even Miss Campbell joined in, in spite of her annoyance.

"I should think you might sing your own songs, Buxton, instead of letting a young lady do it for you," said Mr. Campbell at last.

"Allow me," answered the bachelor calmly.

He seized the guitar, re-tuned it with great care, and began strumming lightly on the strings. Suddenly he lifted up his voice in song and nobody attempted to keep a serious countenance because he seemed entirely oblivious to all jests at his expense. Here is the song he sang:

"A Magnet hung in a hardware shop,
And all around was a loving crop
Of scissors and needles, nails and knives,
Offering love for all their lives;
But for iron the Magnet felt no whim;
Though he charmed iron, it charmed not him;
From needles and nails and knives he'd turn,
For he'd set his heart on a Silver Churn!

"A Silver Churn! A Silver Churn!
His most esthetic
Very magnetic
Fancy took this turn:
If I can wheedle
A knife or a needle,
Why not a Silver Churn?

"And Iron and Steel expressed surprise;
The needles opened their well-drilled eyes,
The penknives felt shut up, no doubt;
The scissors declared themselves cut out.
The kettles, they boiled with rage, 'tis said;
While every nail went off its head
And hither and thither began to roam,
Till a hammer came up and drove them home.

"It drove them home! It drove them home!
While this magnetic,
Peripatetic
Lover, he lived to learn,
By no endeavor
Can a Magnet ever
Attract a Silver Churn!"

"Well, really," cried Mr. Campbell, at the end of the song when the laughter had somewhat died down, "really, I think Buxton, you are the most shameless old soul I ever met in my life. Come along and start home. A shower is coming up, and we'd better get the cars into the valley before it catches us and wets the Silver Churn, and the scissors, and needles, and nails, and knives."

A shower did come up, a big one that lasted most of the way home, and Billie's gray linen suit was wet through, but the weather was warm and except that she looked extremely bedraggled, she was none the worse and refused to accept the loan of Nicholas' coat. They left the three guests in Tokyo with the hired motor car, and Mr. Campbell with Miss Helen and Mary joined the others in the "Comet." So it was that the subject of the raincoat came up again. Miss Campbell, seeing her young cousin's wet suit, exclaimed:

"Child! Where is your raincoat? How often have I told you never to leave it behind, especially in this country where it rains more than it shines."

"It's torn, Cousin Helen," answered Billie meekly.

"But why, pray, didn't you take Nancy's?"

Billie considered a moment what she should say and ended by saying nothing at all.

"Why didn't you borrow Nancy's, Billie?" asked Elinor.

"Nancy didn't seem willing to lend it," answered Billie at last, slowly.

There was a strained silence. Then Miss Campbell remarked:

"I believe the child must be seriously ill. It sounds like typhoid fever. I think we'd better send for the doctor as soon as we reach home."

However, this was not necessary. There was Nancy waiting for them on the piazza. Her headache had gone, she said, and she looked quite well and much more cheerful than usual. She did not notice the faintest tinge of coldness in their greetings. Even Mr. Campbell was not so cordial as usual.

"You must have been caught in the worst of the rain," she said, looking at Billie's dripping clothes.

"We were," put in Mary quickly, trying to cover the silence of the others.

Somehow Billie felt just a bit savage at the moment.

"I've brought you some sacred water from Fujiyama, Nancy," she said presently, in order to hide her hurt feelings.

"Oh, thanks. What am I to do with it? Drink it down?"

"Oh, no. Anoint yourself with it. Sprinkle it over the top of your head for luck."

"Better put on your mackintosh first, Nancy," broke in Elinor coldly. "You'll be wetter than Billie if you don't."

Nancy's face flushed scarlet and she turned and walked into the house without a word.

"Oh, Elinor, I wish you hadn't said that," said Billie. "See how you hurt her."

"She needed to be hurt," replied Elinor. "She needs to be brought to her senses."

All the world was topsy turvy. The Motor Maids were quarreling among themselves and there was mystery in the air. Their happy little kingdom was being destroyed by internecine wars, and for what reason, Billie could not understand. It was inevitable that Mary and Elinor would come over to her side, now, that is, if Nancy persisted in this strange behavior.

That night, lying beside Nancy in the dark, Billie's hand crept out to meet her unhappy friend's. But Nancy's hands were clasped in front of her and she lay quite still, staring at the wall, the most miserable young person in all the universe.

CHAPTER XIX.

FATHER AND DAUGHTER.

The first thing Billie saw next morning when she opened her eyes on a beautiful but heated world, was Nancy seated by the window reading a book, and at a second glance, she recognized it as her own prayer book. If it had been Mary or Elinor who had risen at dawn to read the prayer book, Billie would not have been in the least surprised, for one was deeply religious, and the other also, though she never talked much about it.

Nancy, however, little frivolous butterfly, was not given to reading her testament or prayer book either, except at very infrequent intervals, certainly never early in the morning when other people were asleep. Billie wondered and wondered what more could have happened to turn Nancy's thought into this unusual channel.

"She must be unhappy," she decided, "or she never would have got up at this time of day," and there was a kind of sad humor in the thought which Billie did not appreciate at the moment.

When Nancy heard Billie stir, she closed the book hastily and crept back to bed and Billie pretended not to be awake. She was sure Nancy would rather not have been caught at this act of unusual devotion, and she disliked the idea of being an eavesdropper, as it were, to Nancy's innermost thoughts. Nevertheless, when some time later, Nancy had dressed and gone out of the room, Billie could not resist the temptation to open the prayer book at the purple ribbon; it had been placed at "Prayers for Fair Weather," which begins:

"Almighty and most merciful Father, we humbly beseech thee of thy great goodness to restrain those immoderate rains wherewith for our sins thou hast afflicted us."

Billie could scarcely keep from smiling when she followed Nancy into the dining-room.

"It's about the queerest state of affairs that ever existed," she thought, casting a covert glance at her unhappy friend who was munching dry toast.

Mr. Campbell came in late. He looked flustered and disturbed about something.

"What is the matter with this household?" Billie's thoughts continued. "One would think an earthquake had shaken us out of our senses. Even Papa is out of sorts. I don't think I ever saw him quite this way before. As for me, I can't seem to pull out of the general depression. It's just closing in on us and drawing us down. Papa," she exclaimed out loud, "I believe we need a trip. When are you going to take us to the mountains? Nancy is terribly run down, and Cousin Helen is feeling the heat, and Elinor and Mary and I are going to be run down, too, if you don't hustle us off somewhere."

"Very soon now, daughter. Just one more piece of business to transact and - er - a question to settle, and I'll pack you all off to a cool, dry place."

"It will be the very opposite to this one, then," announced Billie. "Hot and damp are the words to use about Tokyo, and they do say the long rains are coming on - " she stopped short and looked at Nancy.

Everybody was looking at Nancy, in fact.

Mary and Elinor were wondering why Nancy looked so conscious. Miss Campbell was thinking how pale the girl looked, and Mr. Campbell was thinking of something quite

KATHERINE STOKES

different, but very important, concerning Nancy Brown.

Billie tried to cover the uncomfortable silence by adding with a forced cordiality:

"Nancy-Bell needs the change more than any of us."

"Very well, if agreeable to your Royal Highness, I will let you know tonight when we shall break up camp and march for the hills."

"Good," cried Billie. "The Court is prepared to move on a moment's notice."

Mr. Campbell beckoned to his daughter to follow him to his library after breakfast. Billie had already had a foreboding that something was the matter, and she was sure of it as soon as she had entered the room and closed the door.

Her father was standing at his desk frowning as he looked thoughtfully into space, and Mr. Campbell never frowned unless he had something to frown about.

"What's the matter, Papa?"

"Where are the others?"

"Gone to their rooms, I suppose, or in the garden. I didn't notice."

He drew an easy chair up by the open window and Billie took her seat on the arm and rested her cheek against his.

"Papa, is there any trouble brewing in this house?" she asked presently.

Mr. Campbell blew out a long column of smoke from his morning cigar.

"What makes you think so, sweetheart?" he asked.

"I can feel it. It's in the air - it's all about us. It's like a sort of plague. Nancy's got it, and now you are getting it, and I have a feeling I shall catch it, too."

"Has Nancy got it?"

"She got it first and she's giving it to all the rest of us. Oh, Papa, it's the very first time anything like this has ever happened on any of our trips. It's making me quite wretched."

"But what is it, little girl?"

"I don't know, at least, not exactly."

"Not exactly? Then you do know something?"

Billie did not wish to tell her father about the letter Nancy had written. She felt that her father might not take such a charitable view of it as she had, and she had a feeling she must protect poor Nancy, wounded as she had been by her strange behavior.

"Then you do know something?" repeated Mr. Campbell.

"Oh, just the littlest something, but I don't want to tell you, Papa."

Mr. Campbell settled himself into the depths of his chair and drew his arm around his daughter's waist.

"That's right, little daughter. I'd rather you'd be loyal than anything else in the world," he said, stroking her hand. "But I'm going to tell you a little bit of something. I want to ask your advice. I don't know what to do. You must help your old father decide."

"Fire away, Papa."

"Yesterday a very strange thing happened in this house while we were away - a very serious thing, I may say, and one which gives me considerable uneasiness. Last night I came into the library to work, just after dinner. I opened the safe and found that some one had been rummaging among the papers in there."

"Oh, Papa," ejaculated Billie anxiously, knowing the value of those documents.

"They were all there, but they had been disturbed. There had been an attempt made to trace off some of the drawings. The specifications and descriptions had been tampered with, too. I never dreamed such a thing could be managed in the daytime with the house full of servants. The two watchmen would prevent even a possibility of it at night. Whoever did it must have laid his plans well, or else -"

Mr. Campbell paused and looked at his daughter very hard.

"Nancy has been greatly troubled about something lately, hasn't she, little daughter?"

"Yes, Papa, she has, but it's nothing serious," said Billie stoutly. "Just the heat and that absurd business about Yoritomo. You know she did really make eyes at him a good deal."

"Where was she yesterday?"

"In her room, I suppose?"

"Billie, I called several of the servants in last night and questioned them about this business here," he pointed to the safe in the corner. "I called them in separately and each one made the same statement. Nancy spent most of the day in this room."

Billie started.

"I can't believe it. I won't believe it," she cried, rising to her feet in her excitement.

"They told a pretty straight story and they had no reason, as far as I can see, for telling any other kind."

"But what does Nancy know about opening a safe, Papa? It's absurd. And besides what would she want with plans for government improvements or whatever they are?"

"I'm just as much in the dark as you are, Billie. I'm only telling you what O'Haru and Onoye and Komatsu told me. She went into the library twice during the day; once for a little while in the morning, and after lunch when the servants were in the back of the house, Onoye saw her come out of the garden in a pouring rain. She marched straight to this room and locked the door behind her and here she remained until not long before we returned."

"Papa, I'll never go back on Nancy," cried Billie. "I'll never believe she did it - even - well, even if she were to tell me so herself! I know her as well as I know myself. I know all her ins and outs, you might say. She's simply incapable of doing a dishonest thing. Besides, what earthly use could she have with those papers?"

"Do you think she could be doing it for some one else?" asked Mr. Campbell.

"No," burst out Billie, almost angrily. "Why, Papa, I'm ashamed of you,"

Mr. Campbell drew his daughter to him and kissed her.

"You are a good friend, Billie, and I'm going to give your friend the benefit of every doubt in her favor. I'm going to assume that she is innocent and that there is some big mistake somewhere. But I want you to help me because it will be necessary to get at the bottom of the business immediately.

Now, Yoritomo Ito is one great big fanatic. I discovered that the other day when he called here in his foolish garb and demanded the hand of Miss Nancy. He was very angry over being turned down and just a bit threatening in his manner. Of course he resents outside people being called in for the work I am doing. He resents my presence in his country, in fact."

"I don't like him, Papa," broke in Billie, "and - you didn't know that he has been married and divorced?"

Mr. Campbell looked surprised.

"No, indeed, I did not know it. He has colossal nerve, I must say. But divorce is pretty common over here. Most anybody can get one who wants to."

"And, Papa," went on Billie, "I believe that our little maid, Onoye, was his wife, and when her father lost his money, Yoritomo got a divorce, and she and her mother were so poor they had to go to work."

Mr. Campbell was even more shocked at this disclosure.

"And, Papa, I believe she would do most any favor for Yoritomo in order to get to see her little boy who lives with Mme. Ito. Onoye and her mother are mad about him, and - and - " went on Billie, slowly working out the complication in her mind - "they were the ones who laid the blame on Nancy, weren't they?"

"I didn't know I had a detective for a daughter," said Mr. Campbell, smiling.

"I'm just putting two and two together," said Billie. "You see it works out like a jigsaw puzzle."

"So I see," said Mr. Campbell gravely. "There is only one bright spot in the whole business," he added, with something very like a chuckle. "For once in my life I've out-tricked a trickster and I've really enjoyed doing it. Buxton informed me the very night you shot somebody here -"

"There you are," interrupted Billie. "That was Onoye, remember."

"Yes, there is no doubt about that. Well, Buxton informed me that they were after my papers and the safe would be the place they would look for them. So that very night I substituted some old drawings and put the important ones in another place. Now a Japanese, when he's after something, is as crafty and shrewd as a fox. That's why I'm patting myself on my back for having outwitted one."

"Where do you keep the real papers, Papa?"

"Down where the pistol is under some stationery in the back of the desk drawer, and in the big vase in the corner."

Billie went straight to the desk and opened the drawer. She drew out the pistol as she had done that dark night, removed several layers of envelopes and paper, and came at last to a layer of drawings.

"Are these the ones?" she asked, placing them on the desk and then shoving the drawer back with her knee. Something stuck and she pulled it all the way out in her effort to discover what the trouble was. In the very back, caught between the drawer and the framework was a handkerchief. It was small and sheer and in one corner was an embroidered butterfly.

Mr. Campbell jumped up in much excitement.

"By Jove," he exclaimed, "did you find that among my papers?"

Billie nodded her head sadly. "It's Nancy's, too," she said.

Mr. Campbell began looking over the papers.

"She may have dropped her handkerchief," he said, "but I don't think she got down to these. They are exactly as I left them. I suppose she rummaged around with her handkerchief in her lap and it fell in and was shoved back when I took out my papers later."

The papers in a leather portfolio in the vase were safe, also.

For some time the father and daughter sat together, turning over the events of the morning in their minds.

"Papa," said Billie, after a while, "let's send Cousin Helen and Nancy and Elinor to the mountains, because they need the trip more than the rest of us, and suppose you and Mary Price and I stay here and ferret out the whole thing. Of course the person who did it, and I know Nancy had nothing to do with it," she added almost fiercely, "but the real person will be coming back for the rest of the drawings, and that will be our chance. A detective in the house would give the alarm, but Mary and I might turn watchmen without arousing any suspicion, especially if some of the servants are mixed in it."

Mr. Campbell ended by taking his daughter's advice.

The very next morning Miss Campbell and two of the Motor Maids were packed off to Myanoshita, a summer resort in the mountains, with Komatsu to look after them, while the other two Motor Maids remained with Mr. Campbell.

"We'll follow you by the end of the week," he said. "I hope you don't begrudge a lonely man his daughter for that short time, Cousin."

"I hope you won't keep her in this awful heat any longer than you can help," was his cousin's reply. For Miss Campbell had grown to regard Billie as her especial property.

CHAPTER XX.

THE TYPHOON.

The three conspirators had formed no particular plan for a campaign. Mr. Campbell was certain of only one thing: if poor Nancy Brown had foolishly got herself involved in this business, it would be better to keep the secret in the family, as it were.

"We'll just give the child a good lecture and take her home," he said to himself, biting off the end of his cigar and frowning at the disquieting thought. "Whatever she did was through innocence, I am certain of that. She may have been flattered or cajoled into it. Who knows? The little thing is miserable enough without being made more unhappy. I suppose I should have sent for her and asked for a confession, but I hadn't the nerve and that's the truth."

Several uneventful days passed after the departure of the others. It was very hot and the girls kept indoors until after sunset. But it was a dull, dispiriting time, and one morning they decided to take a spin in the "Comet," leaving Mr. Campbell at home to look after things. They had hardly gone when he was summoned to Tokyo by a messenger, and there was no one but the servants left in the house.

The girls motored into town and spent the morning shopping. From one curio shop to another they wandered in the quest of nothing except diversion.

"There is no end to the beautiful things here," sighed Mary, wishing in her heart that she could carry the most beautiful and priceless thing in Tokyo home to her mother.

"Yes, everything is beautiful except the weather," remarked Billie, pointing to the black clouds which had gathered while they were in a shop. "We are going to have one of those red-letter storms, Mary. I think we'd better hurry home as fast as we can."

But the "Comet," who never had any luck all the time he was in Japan, proceeded to burst one of his tires and the explosion mingled threateningly with a low roll of thunder in the distance.

"We'd better take him to a garage and go back in a 'riksha," announced Billie, much annoyed. "Poor old 'Comet,' it wasn't his fault, but the prologues of these storms do put one in a bad temper."

"They frighten me," said Mary. "They give me evil forebodings."

The "Comet" was accordingly left at the garage to be repaired, and the girls were well on their way home in a jinriksha before anything worse had happened than rumblings and strange mutterings at what seemed a great distance away. It sometimes takes hours for a great storm in Japan to reach a head; which, in a way, is rather fortunate, because it gives people a chance to prepare for the struggle. A house is usually completely closed with storm shutters. Not even the smallest opening is left, through which the demon wind can find its way and so carry off the roof, or even the house itself. Every detachable object out of doors is taken inside. The gardener is seen hurrying about protecting his most valuable plants, and by the time the storm bursts upon the scene, filled with demoniacal shrieks and howls like an army of barbarians pursuing the enemy, it finds its victims prepared for the attack.

When the 'riksha turned in at the Campbell gate, it had grown so dark that only the dim outlines of the house were visible at the end of the driveway. No one saw them arrive. The servants were probably at the back putting on the storm shutters, which were all in place at the front.

Billie invited the 'riksha man to go around to the servants' quarters and wait until the storm had passed, but he nodded cheerfully and took his way down the road.

"Let's go in by the passage door," suggested Mary. "Everything is closed up here."

Billie followed her wearily. The heat and oppression were almost beyond endurance. She felt she might be suffocated at any moment. It was like trying to breathe under a feather mattress or in a total vacuum, for that matter.

"Shall we put on our kimonos and lie on the floor in the library?" she suggested as they slipped into the passage. And this they accordingly did without another word or a moment's delay. It was too hot to think or sleep or eat or speak. All they desired was to stretch out on the rug in a cool dark room and keep perfectly still.

There was a deadly quiet in the house when presently two little kimonoed forms stole through the halls and crept to the library door. Billie felt for the knob in the darkness and turned it. The door was locked. In the dense atmosphere it was difficult for them to realize what this meant at first.

"Mary, it's - it's the-what-do-you-call-'em," said Billie incoherently.

Mary nodded silently. She might have shrieked her answer aloud, for the storm had arrived with a great howling of wind and rain, and with flashes of lightning followed by repeated and deafening cannonades of thunder.

The rain rattled on the roof like iron and all the demons in bedlam seemed to be besieging the house. Then a most sickening thing happened. The floor appeared to be heaving under their feet. Doors all over the house banged to with loud reports like revolvers shooting off. There was a crash in the library, a loud cry from within, the door flew open and a figure rushed past. Mary, kneeling on the floor at the threshold, involuntarily reached out her hands and seized the flying skirts of the apparition, or whatever it was, which disappeared like a shadow through the passage door, leaving Mary still holding the substance of the shadow which seemed to be the skirt she had grasped.

A second shock followed almost immediately, less violent than the first but quite as sickening. For one instant the house tossed and pitched like a ship on a choppy sea. Then it settled down on its foundations. Most Japanese houses are built on wooden supports, stout square pillars rounded off at the base and resting in a round socket of stone. This gives a certain elasticity for resisting shocks which a firmly built house would not endure.

The girls lay side by side on the floor of the passage, too frightened to speak. There is a horror about an earthquake that is indescribable to those who have never felt it; a feeling of sickening inefficiency and helplessness.

After a while they plucked up courage to rise and totter weakly into the library, where Billie, her hand shaking with nervous excitement, struck a match and lit a candle. The room was in dire confusion. Chairs were upset, books had fallen off the shelves and lay scattered about the floor, and the iron safe had crashed over on its face. On the desk and the floor about it were numbers of loose sheets of paper and a narrow roll of tracing paper, which had uncoiled itself and lay half on the desk, half on the floor like a long white serpent.

Mechanically they began to put things to rights. Mary gathered up the books and set them back on the shelves and Billie stood the chairs on their legs and collected the papers.

They were not important ones, she knew, only decoys, as her father had called them. In the mean time the house rocked in the clutches of the storm.

"I don't know why we bother to do this," said Billie laughing hysterically. "We may be flying through the air any minute ourselves along with the chairs and papers and everything else."

"The storm at Nikko was mere child's play to this; just an infant babe in arms," answered Mary, weeping softly while she worked.

It seemed better to be doing something than to sit still and listen to the terrifying fury of the tempest, as again and again it hurled itself against the house.

"It wouldn't have done any good even if we had caught the thief or spy or whatever he is," observed Billie after a while. "There would have been no one to help us."

Suddenly Mary's perturbed mind harked back to what had happened in the hall.

"Billie," she cried, "it wasn't a man; it was a woman. That skirt I caught - that - that something - where is it?"

"What are you talking about, Mary?"

"I tell you I caught hold of something. It came off in my hands."

She ran into the hall and, groping about on the floor, presently found what seemed to be a long coat. Rushing back she spread it on the desk. Billie held the candle high and the two girls stood gazing at it for some moments without speaking. Then Billie slowly placed the candle on the desk and sat down.

"I don't understand, Billie," said Mary, clasping and unclasping her hands in her excitement and surprise, "it's

Nancy's blue raincoat, but - but I don't understand."

Billie covered her eyes with one hand as if she would like to hide from Mary what they might tell of her feelings and thoughts. There was nothing to say. It *was* Nancy's blue raincoat, but she refused to think what the explanation might be.

After a long time, it seemed, O'Haru came into the room. She was amazed to find the girls in the library until they explained how they had just escaped the storm.

"Oh, much terrible," ejaculated the housekeeper. "Much terrible more worse than since," from which they gathered that it was one of the worst storms ever seen in Tokyo. O'Haru brought in lights and presently returned at the head of a procession of maids with trays of food; though whether it was luncheon or supper time it was impossible to tell. The clocks had all stopped in the earthquake and it was still as black as night. It might have been midnight or midday for all they knew.

The girls preferred to remain in the library, which seemed to them more protection than the other rooms, and O'Haru drew up three tables and arranged the trays with great deftness and celerity.

"Papa didn't come?" asked Billie, noticing the third table.

"No, honorable lady."

"For whom is the other tray, then?"

"Mees Brown," answered O'Haru, rather surprised.

"But she is in the mountains," said Billie, growing very red and uneasy. "Oh, Nancy, Nancy," she groaned inwardly, "could it have really been you and are you out there in the typhoon?"

"Pardon grant," said O'Haru. "Mees Brown arriving at

morning. Mees Brown within."

"I think not, O'Haru," said Billie.

"Her honorable rainy coat," said Onoye, pointing to the fated blue mackintosh.

"Mary, what shall I say?" asked Billie in a low voice. "I don't know what to do."

"Ask them questions," said Mary.

From Onoye they gathered that Miss Brown had arrived soon after Mr. Campbell had left the house, and had gone straight to her room. She was very tired, she said, and would lie down until lunch time. Then she had gone to the library. Just before the storm they had tried to go in and close the shutters, but had found the door locked.

Billie formed a resolution to protect Nancy no matter what was to pay.

"It wasn't the real Miss Brown," she announced firmly. "It was some one dressed like her. The real Miss Brown is far away from here in the mountains."

The two Japanese women withdrew presently, and if they felt any curiosity about Nancy's strange appearance at the villa, they were careful to hide it.

The storm lasted all night and many times the two girls lying side by side on Billie's bed were prepared for the house to fall on top of them or to be carried away on the wind like chips of wood. But toward morning the wind died down and while the rain continued to flood the earth, they knew the worst was over. Billie drew back the bolts of their storm shutters and the fresh air came pouring in to revive their drooping spirits.

"Mary," she said, creeping back to bed, "I'll never believe it was Nancy. No, never, never."

At last they went to sleep, and when they waked the rain had ceased altogether. The lawn in front of the house was a muddy lake and many trees lay prone on the ground. It was a scene of devastation that greeted Mr. Campbell as he hurried home at daylight in a 'riksha. He had dispatched a messenger in the night, paying a large fee, to see if the girls were safe at home and had spent the night in Tokyo with Mr. Buxton.

It was not until much later in the day that Billie plucked up courage to inform her father of what had happened.

"Why on earth didn't you tell me about it immediately?" he exclaimed. "The best way to settle that, is to telegraph to Cousin Helen right off."

But with the "Comet" in town and Komatsu in the mountains this was not so easy to manage, and it looked as if Mr. Campbell would have to walk back to Tokyo. He had got half way down the drive, in fact, when a messenger appeared running at full speed as fast as a horse; such is the endurance of a Japanese runner. He had been sent with a telegram from Mr. Campbell's office, but it had been written in Japanese and had to be translated.

Mr. Campbell hurried back to the house and called Onoye:

"Read this for me if you can," he ordered.

Onoye looked at the strange script a long time. Then she read slowly:

"'O'Nainci San gone Tokyo. No honorable telling before for why she make those journey -'"

There were a few more words, but Onoye had reached the limit of her knowledge of the English language.

Mr. Campbell sighed. Billie was the only girl in the world who wasn't any trouble, he thought.

KATHERINE STOKES

CHAPTER XXI.

CONUNDRUMS AND ANSWERS.

"I tell you Nancy is on her way, now, Papa," said Billie emphatically. "She would never have had time to get here as soon as yesterday. The storm would have delayed her. She couldn't have reached here."

Mr. Campbell shook his head anxiously as he paced up and down the piazza waiting for the 'riksha the messenger was to send back from Tokyo.

Billie's faith in her friend was wonderful. He admired it, but he was obliged to say he felt rather skeptical himself, all things considered.

"There comes the 'riksha," announced Mary at last.

Mr. Campbell went into the house for his hat and cane and Billie followed him. She looked so pale and miserable that he stooped to kiss her and then led her into the library.

"Come in here a moment, little daughter," he said, "and we'll talk things over a bit."

"How are you going to find her, Papa?" Billie asked, wiping away the tears that would well in her eyes every few minutes and trickle down her cheeks.

"I'll do everything within human power. The police are excellent and so are the detectives."

"Why do you think she ran away?" sobbed Billie, breaking down entirely.

"I don't know, my child. I can't make out what the reason was and we'd never get anywhere by guessing."

"Papa, do you think she could have gone to that widow? I never told you, but she did once before when we had a quarrel. She was awfully sorry after the first night and came back."

Mr. Campbell gave a low whistle. He had forgotten the Widow of Shanghai's very existence until that moment.

"I hope she's there. That will make it much simpler. But you mustn't take on so, little daughter. Nancy is like lots of headstrong girls. She resents criticism. Probably she had a falling out with Cousin Helen and ran away -"

"I did run away," said a voice at the door, "but that wasn't the reason."

"Nancy!" cried Billie and the two girls rushed into each other's arms and embraced like sisters long separated. In the doorway stood Mary and Mr. Buxton. Mary's face was beaming with joy and Mr. Buxton wore his old expression of humorous tolerance.

"Where did you find her, Buxton?" asked Mr. Campbell gravely.

"I didn't find her. She found me this morning at an unconscionably early hour, too, and a fine time we've had of it, I can tell you. We've chased a widow back to Shanghai and we've placed a fanatic under bond for good behavior."

Nancy laughed her old natural laugh with a ripple of gaiety in it. Her eyes were sparkling and the color flooded her cheeks. She was prettier than ever, it seemed, and all because she was so happy! Her jaunty little traveling hat was over one eye and her dress was crushed and wrinkled, but her charming face was radiant.

"The morning we left for the mountains," she began, "two letters came for me by mail but I didn't read them until I got on the train. One of them was from that awful woman and it frightened me terribly. It seemed cordial enough on the surface but my eyes have been opened to her. I don't know just what she is, but she is dangerous I am certain, - like a cat ready to spring. She said she had taken such a fancy to me that she must see me again and she thought it would be advisable for me to come to her home at once. The other letter was from that horrid Yoritomo and he simply threatened in so many words to blow up the house and everybody in it unless I listened to him. I didn't think much about the letters until we were settled in the hotel. Then I began to get more and more uneasy and I thought the best thing for me to do was to come back to Tokyo and see Mr. Campbell. I knew, of course, that Miss Helen would never let me go alone, so I just ran away."

"And very glad we are to see you, Miss Nancy," broke in Mr. Campbell in the tone of one who felt enormously relieved.

"We were all night on the train," continued Nancy. "The storm had washed the track away in places and we had to wait many times while it was repaired. As soon as I arrived, I took a 'riksha to Mr. Buxton's lodgings and then we went to see Mme. Fontaine and Yoritomo -"

"Oh, that widow woman," interrupted Mr. Buxton. "She's a sly one, I can tell you. As we entered the front door, she departed at the back. We left several policemen waiting for her to return but I wouldn't be surprised if she were well on her way to Shanghai by now."

"I don't understand," said Billie.

"The time we quarreled, Billie, and I behaved like such a silly little goose," Nancy explained, "you remember I went to see her. I don't know what made me do it, except that I wanted to air my troubles. I've been so unhappy since, that I feel years older now. I was only a child then, but I'm quite an old person now. She talked to me a long time that night and got me all stirred up and believing that I had been badly treated. It was not what she really said but what she hinted. She seemed to know a good deal about Mr. Campbell's work. She implied that what he was doing for the Japanese government was disloyal to America. I was so fascinated with the way she put things and the way she looked at me, too, that I didn't seem to have any power over myself any more. It was like being hypnotized, I suppose. It came into my head to write you a terrible letter, Billie, -" Nancy's eyes filled with tears and her voice choked - "I can hardly think of it now without crying. She knew I was writing it but she didn't ask what was in it, only occasionally, while I wrote, she would look over at me and say 'Poor darling! Poor pretty darling!' After I got to bed, I came to my senses and began to realize what I had done. I was terribly frightened and unhappy and in the middle of the night I crept into the drawing-room, tore up the letter and threw the pieces into a vase. Next morning, you remember, I came home. But the letter was so heavy on my conscience, I couldn't be happy. I had a feeling it had never been destroyed and would somehow get to you, Billie. I wrote to the widow and asked her to send me back the pieces if she could find them, so that I could burn them myself. In her reply, she simply said the vase was empty and I gradually began to understand that she had got the letter and intended to keep it. There was a threatening sound to the note, and she ended by asking to borrow my blue raincoat. I had to let her have it, but I knew she didn't want it for any good reason and I was more and more miserable. I began to pray that it wouldn't rain. People don't wear raincoats in good weather. I tried to argue with myself about her reasons for wanting my raincoat and even now I don't know what they were unless it was to involve me in something. But we've frightened her away, anyhow, and she can have the raincoat if she'll only stay."

"She certainly did want to get you into a peck of trouble, Miss

Nancy," said Mr. Campbell bringing the famous raincoat from the passage where it hung on the hat rack. "Here's your coat. She left it behind as a souvenir yesterday when she broke into the house to steal my drawings. I fooled her, though," he added, smiling sweetly. "If she thinks she can ever make anything out of those papers, she'll soon find she has been losing time."

"It's the third time she's been here masquerading as you, Nancy." broke in Billie. "She must have managed the disguise perfectly because the servants were fooled each time."

"She did," said Mary. "I asked Onoye exactly what she looked like. She evidently had on a brown curly wig and a hat like Nancy's with a blue veil around her head."

At this juncture in the conversation, Onoye announced a visitor who proved to be a detective. He was a quiet, self-contained young Japanese who spoke excellent English. He had been sent out in a motor car by the Chief of Police to find out all he could from the Americans regarding Mme. Fontaine.

The Widow of Shanghai, he informed them, was the child of a Russian father and a Japanese mother. She was considered to be one of the most accomplished and brilliant spies in the Orient and could assume almost any disguise and speak most languages. It was a pity a woman of such wonderful talents should stoop to work like that, and the strange part of it was that she was sometimes treacherous to Russia and in favor of Japan: so that it was difficult to tell for which side she worked. Just now her sympathies were with Russia, since she was trying to get plans for harbor defenses in Japan. The Chief of Police wished to thank Miss Brown in behalf of the City of Tokyo for driving the so-called Mme. Fontaine out of town. She had entered it so quietly that until that very morning it was not known that Mme. Fontaine and the famous Russian spy were one and the same person.

"Of course it was she who was in here the night of your

birthday party. Papa," said Billie. "I must have shot two people instead of one."

This was actually the case, as Onoye explained to her later. Onoye had hidden herself behind the curtain that night to watch the couples strolling about in the moonlight. Mme. Fontaine came very swiftly into the room and blew out the lights. She carried a little electric dark lantern. Onoye was too frightened to make her presence known, and had crept along the edge of the room hoping to reach the door. Then Billie had come in and somehow they had all drifted together in the dark and the pistol had gone off. The bullet must have pierced Mme. Fontaine's arm and lodged in Onoye's wrist. How she managed to hide the wound with a scarf until she got her long wrap from one of the bedrooms was a marvel to them all.

"Anyhow the mystery is all cleared away now," cried Nancy joyfully. "I suppose you must have thought strange things about me, Mr. Campbell?"

"We had every reason to think them, Miss Nancy, but this loyal young person here wouldn't let us. It looked like some pretty convincing evidence for a while, but she wouldn't budge from the stand she had taken."

Once again the two friends embraced. They were radiantly happy. It was just as if Nancy had died and come to life again.

"I think I've learned a good lesson," she admitted at last. "It all happened because I wanted to be silly and romantic and meet people in the garden and write notes."

"People?" asked Mary.

Nancy laughed and dimpled in her old charming way and everybody laughed, even the reserved young detective. Old Nedda, who had followed them into the room, carne tottering over to where Nancy sat beside Billie. The aged animal whined and wagged her tail, as if she, too, wished to take part in the general thanksgiving.

"Dearest old great-grandmama," cried Nancy, kneeling beside the aged pug and hiding her face in the tawny coat, "are you really glad to see me, too?"

CHAPTER XXII.

GOOD-BYE, SUMMER.

A string of glowing lanterns festooned the piazza of the Campbell villa, while within the warm reflection of wood fires and shaded lamps made each window a square of hospitable brightness. The house inside was a blaze of color. Splendid bunches of scarlet maple leaves and chrysanthemums of amazing size and beauty filled the vases and jars.

The Motor Maids, dressed in their very best party frocks, had gathered in the drawing-room early before the arrival of the three guests. Each maid sat in a large chair and gazed about her from side to side. The riot of color, the scarlets and oranges, the tawny browns, pale pinks and delicate yellows seemed to bewilder them.

"I suppose it wasn't truly Japanese to decorate a room with all these masses of flowers and leaves," said Billie. "But I don't care. It's the most gorgeous thing I've ever seen and since this is our last night here we want to make it a festive one."

Their last night! Was it possible that time had slipped by so fast? Here it was already November, the season of greatest beauty in Japan, when Nature has dipped her brush into the most brilliant colors on the palette and touched the foliage with red and gold, the skies with deepest blue, and the chrysanthemums, favorite flower of the Emperor, with every gorgeous shade.

After a good rest in the mountains broken by excursions to

various interesting places about the country, the Campbell party had returned to Tokyo in time to marvel at the wonders of the chrysanthemum festival, which is a national affair.

Away off at the other side of the world a certain High School was now in full swing. But even Mary Price had lost all scruples concerning her education.

"I don't care," she remarked recklessly. "I think all this beauty is just as good for the mind as bare plastered walls and plain geometry."

"It's better," exclaimed Nancy, "because it makes one so much happier to look at chrysanthemums and red maples than to try and understand why the sum of the three angles of a triangle of any old size must always equal two right angles. What makes one happy is far more educational than what makes one aggravated."

Here was a Pagan theory that Elinor felt inclined to doubt.

"We shall have to study double time all during the Christmas holidays," she said.

"It will be rather fun, I think," put in Billie, always the optimist of the quartette. "We'll all just have a small private school of four and jump in and work together. To me, working together is almost as nice as playing together. I suppose I appreciate it more than the rest of you because I had to work and play alone for so many years."

"Billie, you are a perfect dear," ejaculated Nancy. "You furnish all the amusement and fun and thank us for sharing it with you."

Billie looked as pleased and happy as if she had never had a compliment before in her life. The joy of having regained Nancy after that brief eclipse into shadow was still too recent to be forgotten. The two girls exchanged one of those telegraphic glances of intimate friends who need no words to express their meaning.

"We've had a wonderful time," broke in Mary. "There is something about the land that makes one forget the realities. If poor little Kenkyo hadn't died -"

"Be careful! Onoye is in the next room," interrupted Billie, lifting a warning finger.

Onoye had indeed been the wife of Yoritomo as Billie had guessed. No doubt it was poor old O'Haru who had thrown the stone into the summer house that day. Billie had mercifully never inquired. And now the little son, for whom the two women had yearned with a passion that is extraordinarily deep in Japanese women, had been gathered to his forefathers. Onoye was dumb and silent with misery during his brief illness. When he died, she had disappeared for a few days and returned at last calm and still. No one had seen her shed a tear. Yoritomo, it was said, was stricken with the wildest grief. But sorrow had cleared his brain and brought him to his senses. He had made a really manly apology to Mr. Campbell and had even asked that Onoye might be restored to him. But this was not to be. Miss Campbell had taken Onoye under her wing.

"I want you to go back to America with me and be educated, child," said the kind little lady, "and after a few years, you may return to Japan and teach the women here how to be independent."

Onoye had joyfully and gratefully consented to this arrangement, providing she might act as Miss Campbell's maid in the meantime.

O'Haru had made an heroic effort to be glad, also. She would continue to be the Spears' housekeeper, she said, and wait for her daughter to return to Japan with "muchly honorable learning."

During the hot weeks when Miss Campbell and the Motor Maids were sojourning in the mountains, old "great grand-mama Nedda" had also passed into another sphere. Her ending was peaceful, they said; she had slipped quietly away one day at sunset. The faithful servants buried the gentle creature in the garden not far from the shrine of the Compassionate God. When the girls returned they set up a little wooden monument in her memory on which Mary printed in India ink the following inscription:

"NEDDA"

Died August 27, 19 -

Aged 21.

"Our birth is but a sleep and a forgetting;
The Soul that rises with us, our life's Star,
Hath had elsewhere its setting And cometh from afar."

"Here comes someone," announced Billie, peering from the window of the drawing-room. "It's Mr. Buxton, I think, and he's heavily laden with parcels, apparently."

In another moment, the bachelor himself stood in the doorway regarding the charming picture with his half-humorous, half-grave expression.

"There were only three Graces, were there not?" he asked. "I've forgotten. It's been so long since I met them. But there should have been four."

"And why not five, since you are adding to the number," asked Mary.

"Meaning for the fifth the beauteous lady who lingers in her room?" he demanded.

"She out-graces us all," exclaimed Billie. "But what did you bring with you? Do tell us. We are dying of curiosity."

The bachelor's lips twitched with a crafty smile and he shook one finger at them like the sly old comedian he was.

"Wait!" he said, disappearing into the hall and reappearing in a moment with an aged, gnarled dwarf apple tree growing in a green vase, and a lacquered box beautifully inlaid with mother-of-pearl.

"Do you think I have the ghost of a chance?" he asked them in a whisper.

The girls were consumed with giggles.

"Not the ghost," laughed Billie. "She wouldn't stay in Japan, not if you brought her all the Emperor's chrysanthemums in a single bunch."

"But what's in the box, Mr. Buxton?" demanded Nancy.

"You shall see," he answered. "Wait until the Fifth Grace appears."

"Here she is," they cried in a chorus, as Miss Campbell swept into the room, resplendent in mauve satin covered with billows of fine lace.

"Madame, you blind me with your magnificence," exclaimed the bachelor, making a low bow.

"I'm glad you like my dress," said the elegant little lady.

"It's not the dress but the eyes," he corrected her, just as Mr. Campbell, followed by Reggie Carlton and Nicholas Grimm, appeared.

"We meet to meet again," cried Nicholas, joyfully.

KATHERINE STOKES

The two young men were sailing for America on the same ship with the Campbells, and many a long happy day they were all to have together.

"And I am to be the only figure left on the Japanese screen," said Mr. Buxton sadly. "I shall have to walk across the curved bridges alone and consume tea for two under the flowering cherry tree."

"I am afraid you will, sir," said Miss Campbell.

"Madam, permit me," he said solemnly, placing the apple tree at her feet. "Is this any inducement?"

"Not the slightest," answered Miss Helen with a laugh.

Mr. Buxton gazed sadly from one smiling face to another.

Then he opened the lacquered box and presented each of the Motor Maids with a beautiful embroidered silk robe.

"Have an empty box, then, Madam," he announced, placing the casket in her lap, and because of the riotous and unseemly laughter, no one heard her reply.

So ended the last day of the Motor Maids in their pretty Japanese villa. It was as happy and beautiful an evening as that land of flowers and hospitality could make it. We should not be sorry ourselves to linger with them on those lovely shores, but the winter is at land and the season of dreams has passed.

Komatsu and O'Haru and old Saiki, the gardener, the four little maids, the grandmothers and the children remain picturesque figures in a picturesque land; and behind them, glistening In the sunlight, looms Fujiyama, sacred mountain of dazzling whiteness and perfect beauty.

For the Motor Maids this memory will live as the type of all the experiences and scenes of fair Japan. Above the remembrance of stormy crises - within and without - of their sojourn there, rises the happy consciousness of a firmer, larger friendship which they may take with them as the choicest souvenir of the summer.

And in their homeland, if we wish, we may join them again to find what another year of life has revealed to them. In the meantime, let us anticipate the pleasure in store for us with "The Motor Maids at Sunrise Camp."

Choose from Thousands of 1stWorldLibrary Classics By

Adolphus WilliamWard
Aesop
Agatha Christie
Alexander Aaronsohn
Alexander Kielland
Alexandre Dumas
Alfred Gatty
Alfred Ollivant
Alice Duer Miller
Alice Turner Curtis
Alice Dunbar
Ambrose Bierce
Amelia E. Barr
Andrew Lang
Andrew McFarland Davis
Anna Sewell
Annie Besant
Annie Hamilton Donnell
Annie Payson Call
Anton Chekhov
Arnold Bennett
Arthur Conan Doyle
Arthur Ransome
Atticus
B. M. Bower
Basil King
Bayard Taylor
Ben Macomber
Booth Tarkington
Bram Stoker
C. Collodi
C. E. Orr
C. M. Ingleby
Carolyn Wells
Catherine Parr Traill
Charles A. Eastman
Charles Dickens
Charles Dudley Warner
Charles Farrar Browne
Charles Ives
Charles Kingsley
Charles Lathrop Pack
Charles Whibley
Charles Willing Beale
Charlotte M. Braeme
Charlotte M.Yonge
Clair W. Hayes
Clarence Day Jr.
Clarence E. Mulford

Clemence Housman
Confucius
Cornelis DeWitt Wilcox
Cyril Burleigh
D. H. Lawrence
Daniel Defoe
David Garnett
Don Carlos Janes
Donald Keyhole
Dorothy Kilner
Dougan Clark
E. Nesbit
E.P.Roe
E. Phillips Oppenheim
Edgar Allan Poe
Edgar Rice Burroughs
Edith Wharton
Edward J. O'Biren
John Cournos
Edwin L. Arnold
Eleanor Atkins
Elizabeth Cleghorn
Gaskell
Elizabeth Von Arnim
Ellem Key
Emily Dickinson
Erasmus W. Jones
Ernie Howard Pie
Ethel Turner
Ethel Watts Mumford
Eugenie Foa
Eugene Wood
Evelyn Everett-Green
Everard Cotes
F. J. Cross
Federick Austin Ogg
Ferdinand Ossendowski
Francis Bacon
Francis Darwin
Frances Hodgson Burnett
Frank Gee Patchin
Frank Harris
Frank Jewett Mather
Frank L. Packard
Frederick Trevor Hill
Frederick Winslow Taylor
Friedrich Kerst
Friedrich Nietzsche
Fyodor Dostoyevsky

Gabrielle E. Jackson
Garrett P. Serviss
Gaston Leroux
George Ade
Geroge Bernard Shaw
George Ebers
George Eliot
George MacDonald
George Orwell
George Tucker
George W. Cable
George Wharton James
Gertrude Atherton
Grace E. King
Grant Allen
Guillermo A. Sherwell
Gulielma Zollinger
Gustav Flaubert
H. A. Cody
H. B. Irving
H. G. Wells
H. H. Munro
H. Irving Hancock
H. Rider Haggard
H. W. C. Davis
Hamilton Wright Mabie
Hans Christian Andersen
Harold Avery
Harold McGrath
Harriet Beecher Stowe
Harry Houidini
Helent Hunt Jackson
Helen Nicolay
Hendy David Thoreau
Henrik Ibsen
Henry Adams
Henry Ford
Henry Frost
Henry James
Henry Jones Ford
Henry Seton Merriman
Henry Wadsworth
Longfellow
Henry W Longfellow
Herbert A. Giles
Herbert N. Casson
Herman Hesse
Homer
Honore De Balzac

Horace Walpole
Horatio Alger, Jr.
Howard Pyle
Howard R. Garis
Hugh Lofting
Hugh Walpole
Humphry Ward
Ian Maclaren
Israel Abrahams
J.G.Austin
J. Henri Fabre
J. M. Barrie
J. Macdonald Oxley
J. S. Knowles
J. Storer Clouston
Jack London
Jacob Abbott
James Allen
James Lane Allen
James Andrews
James Baldwin
James DeMille
James Joyce
James Oliver Curwood
James Oppenheim
James Otis
Jane Austen
Jens Peter Jacobsen
Jerome K. Jerome
John Burroughs
John F. Kennedy
John Gay
John Glasworthy
John Habberton
John Joy Bell
John Milton
John Philip Sousa
Jonathan Swift
Joseph Carey
Joseph Conrad
Joseph Jacobs
Julian Hawthrone
Julies Vernes
Justin Huntly McCarthy
Kakuzo Okakura
Kenneth Grahame
Kate Langley Bosher
L. A. Abbot
L. T. Meade
L. Frank Baum
Laura Lee Hope

Laurence Housman
Leo Tolstoy
Leonid Andreyev
Lewis Carroll
Lilian Bell
Lloyd Osbourne
Louis Tracy
Louisa May Alcott
Lucy Fitch Perkins
Lucy Maud Montgomery
Lydia Miller Middleton
Lyndon Orr
M. H. Adams
Margaret E. Sangster
Margaret Vandercook
Maria Edgeworth
Maria Thompson Daviess
Mariano Azuela
Marion Polk Angellotti
Mark Overton
Mark Twain
Mary Austin
Mary Cole
Mary Rowlandson
Mary Wollstonecraft
Shelley
Max Beerbohm
Myra Kelly
Nathaniel Hawthrone
O. F. Walton
Oscar Wilde
Owen Johnson
P.G.Wodehouse
Paul and Mable Thorn
Paul G. Tomlinson
Paul Severing
Peter B. Kyne
Plato
R. Derby Holmes
R. L. Stevenson
Rabindranath Tagore
Rahul Alvares
Ralph Waldo Emmerson
Rene Descartes
Rex E. Beach
Richard Harding Davis
Richard Jefferies
Robert Barr
Robert Frost
Robert Gordon Anderson
Robert L. Drake

Robert Lansing
Robert Michael Ballantyne
Robert W. Chambers
Rosa Nouchette Carey
Ross Kay
Rudyard Kipling
Samuel B. Allison
Samuel Hopkins Adams
Sarah Bernhardt
Selma Lagerlof
Sherwood Anderson
Sigmund Freud
Standish O'Grady
Stanley Weyman
Stella Benson
Stephen Crane
Stewart Edward White
Stijn Streuvels
Swami Abhedananda
Swami Parmananda
T. S. Ackland
The Princess Der Ling
Thomas A. Janvier
Thomas A Kempis
Thomas Anderton
Thomas Bailey Aldrich
Thomas Bulfinch
Thomas De Quincey
Thomas H. Huxley
Thomas Hardy
Thomas More
Thornton W. Burgess
U. S. Grant
Valentine Williams
Victor Appleton
Virginia Woolf
Walter Scott
Washington Irving
Wilbur Lawton
Wilkie Collins
Willa Cather
Willard F. Baker
William Makepeace
Thackeray
William W. Walter
Winston Churchill
Yei Theodora Ozaki
Young E. Allison
Zane Grey

www.ingramcontent.com/pod-product-compliance
Lightning Source LLC
Chambersburg PA
CBHW030316180626
46810CB00003B/1105